"What Do You Want?"

she asked bitterly. "Why are you calling? Can't you leave me alone?"

"No, I can't. Besides, you don't want me to. Now, get dressed. I'll be up in fifteen minutes and we're going to get a few things cleared up."

"No!"

"You heard me. I'll give you fifteen minutes to get ready."

"Go find your secretary. You're not Superman, you know. Take care of one girl at a time. Besides, I'm just not your type."

"And just what is my type?"

"Someone who knows the rules to your silly games. Someone who can be bought as easily as you can buy. I mean it, Travis! Just leave me alone!"

RITA CLAY

has tried almost every job once. This former bookstore manager also sold cosmetics, worked in a bank and ran her own modeling school before turning to writing. Her sense of humor is reflected in her books, along with all the love she has known from her husband and four children.

Dear Reader:

At Silhouette we try to publish books with you, our reader, in mind, and we're always trying to think of something new. We're very pleased to announce the creation of Silhouette First Love, a new line of contemporary romances written by the very finest young adult writers especially for our twelve-to-sixteen-year-old readers. First Love has many of the same elements you've enjoyed in Silhouette Romances—love stories, happy endings and the same attention to detail and description—but features heroines and situations with which our younger readers can more easily identify.

First Love from Silhouette will be available in bookstores this October. We will introduce First Love with six books, and each month thereafter we'll bring you two new First Love romances.

We welcome any suggestions or comments, and I invite you to write to us at the address below.

Karen Solem
Editor-in-Chief
Silhouette Books
P.O. Box 769
New York, N.Y. 10019

RITA CLAY
Wanderer's Dream

Silhouette Romance

Published by Silhouette Books New York

America's Publisher of Contemporary Romance

SILHOUETTE BOOKS, a Simon & Schuster Division of
GULF & WESTERN CORPORATION
1230 Avenue of the Americas, New York. N.Y. 10020

ISBN: 0-671-57097-8

First Silhouette printing August, 1981

10 9 8 7 6 5 4 3 2 1

Map by Tony Ferrara

SILHOUETTE, SILHOUETTE ROMANCE and colophon are
trademarks of Simon & Schuster.

America's Publisher of Contemporary Romance

Printed in the U.S.A.

To Jim, for his pride, encouragement and love.

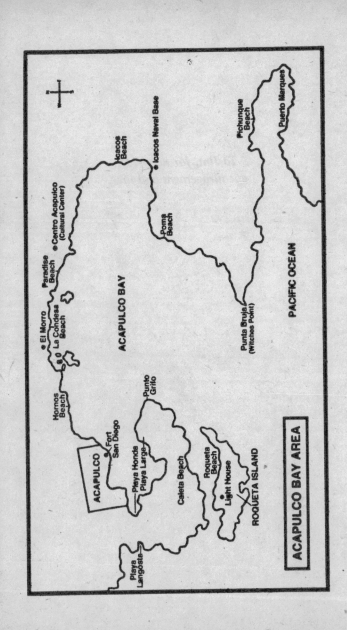

ACAPULCO BAY AREA

Chapter One

This was really happening; it wasn't a dream! Dannee Hathaway checked her seat belt to ensure that it was still fastened securely around her slim waist, her hands shaking with nervous excitement. This was her first plane trip and an excited giggle was doing its best to force its way through her rosebud-shaped mouth.

In an attempt to remain calm and composed, at least in appearance, she turned to view the terrain from the plane window. Hills rose and valleys gently dipped in rich verdant green to shadowed black. The clear, pale blue sky seemed more like a photograph from a travel brochure than reality. There were no towns or villages that she could see, just the great stretch of uneven land that reminded her of a relief map made by schoolchildren and put together with plaster and paste and colored with the clear, pure greens and blues that children love.

The plane banked to the right and the ocean immediately came into view on the left as they followed the coastline to the Acapulco Airport where the plane slowly descended toward the ground. Dannee was mesmerized by the shadow of the plane outlined on the sandy beach below as it sped toward its final destination.

She had never thought she would see anything as wonderful as this in a million years. Acapulco! A wonderland, a passport to another world where playboys played and women were beautiful with their movie-star tans. The lost, lush tropical garden of Adam and Eve couldn't have been more beautiful. All sorts of wonderful things could happen to a girl here. . . .

The pilot's voice filled the cabin with what she assumed were the usual statistics: the temperature, weather conditions, and the "hope you have enjoyed your flight" routine. Dannee smiled as she glanced around the crowded cabin. She seemed to be the only person listening to his monologue.

The plane touched down, bumped up again and then made solid contact with the runway. The whine of the brakes grew louder until the slowdown was complete and they taxied to a stop. The other travelers began reaching for their hand luggage and coats, talking among themselves and pushing into the narrow aisle that led to the exit. She waited a few moments before standing to reach toward the storage area above her seat for the short tan jacket that matched her crisp new tan and white dress, her eyes bright at all the action around her.

She was going first-class on this trip. No sleeping in small out-of-the way motels, no "one meal a day" plan. This was going to be five days of living just like the jet-setters who flew around the world and became bored unless every day was filled with adventures. Opportunities like this only came once in a lifetime and Dannee was going to make the most of it.

She stood quietly by her seat, waiting for the line of pushing people in the aisle to break so she could squeeze into an opening. She glanced around at a few of the more sophisticated women, then tried to mimic them by looking bored and slightly jaded. She tried, but her darting brown eyes, constantly turning to take in the view through the small window, gave her away. She was just too excited to be blasé.

She looked out the window to see how far she had to walk to the terminal just as a large bus attached itself to the exit door. It looked like some great yawning bug as its front touched the side of the plane and hydraulically raised itself up to fit the door. When she reached the exit and stepped into the front of the vehicle, she looked around in delight. It was more like a lobby than a bus. So these were the passenger carriers, designed to shuttle people between the plane and the terminal, she had read about! She gave a sigh of delight as she took one of the seats and looked around the bright, clean vehicle. Everything was new; everything was different. Everything looked like the beginning of an exciting vacation.

The bus slowly backed away from the plane, heading toward the shelter of the terminal. Within seconds, the motor was cut off and the front doors opened to allow the passengers to enter customs. Everything was done in a quick and orderly fashion and before Dannee knew it she was outside in the heat and sunshine, hailing one of the many taxis lined up at the terminal entrance. She handed her luggage to the driver and was helped inside the battered old American car. The driver, a weathered and smiling older man, began yelling greetings to everyone in his gruff voice as they turned down the palm tree lined drive toward Acapulco, some eleven miles away.

She held onto her seat, although his speed was not half as fast as his driving techniques were brazen. A winding road snaked in front of them, following the ups and downs of the terrain. Every once in awhile she could catch a glimpse of the blue Pacific between the trees and it was breathtaking. The driver passed cars without seeming to care that another car might be coming from the opposite direction.

"Do you know where the Acapulco Princess Hotel is, *señor?*" she asked, swaying in her seat as he narrowly passed another car.

"*Sí, señorita. La Princesa,* it is just down the road. Do not worry. I will have you there, *pronto.*"

"But will I arrive all in one piece?" she muttered to herself as she was pitched to one side. He took another sharp curve and she was thrown against the door, hitting her shoulder against the handle with a thud.

"Ouch!"

The driver glanced over his shoulder, surprised to find her on the opposite side of the car from where she had been last. His grin was contagious, if not slightly sheepish. "Forgive me, *señorita.* There was a small dog on the road that did not move fast enough, so I had to dodge him. You would not like me to hit him, would you?"

"Oh, no. Kill the passenger, save the dog, that's my motto," she muttered as she rubbed her shoulder. "But I doubt if Fido will pay my fare when I'm gone." But she had to grin; he was busy telling her the sad stories of his relatives, each of whom had at one time hurt some part of his or her anatomy through falls and freak accidents.

A short while later he let out a sigh. "Ahh, here we are, *señorita.* It is *muy bueno, sí?*"

"*Sí!*" she breathed. They had turned into a palm tree lined drive with flowering bushes of red and purple and several varieties of ferns arranged geometrically on the esplanade.

They went much more slowly now because of
the speed bumps that were spaced all the way
up the drive to the towering pyramid that
posed as a hotel. On both sides of the road,
just beyond the tall palms, was a golf course.
Condominiums and sparkling white cottages
nestled among the tall tropical trees that lined
the fairways. It looked like something from
the movies, almost too beautiful to be real.

On a slight incline ahead of them stood the
Acapulco Princess, built like an ancient pyramid and situated between the white sands of
the beach and the tropical wonderland of the
gardens. They swung around the circular
drive and stopped directly in front of the
porticoed entrance. A bellboy, much older
than the American variety, stepped down the
curb and waited for the driver to open the
trunk, grinning at Dannee's exclamation of
awe.

The entire first floor of the lobby was open to
the elements in the front and rear; no walls or
doors were to be seen. The tiled floor seemed
to stretch forever, covered here and there
with soft, colorfully woven rugs and even
more comfortable-looking couches and chairs
grouped into cozy conversation areas. On
either side of the lobby were twin circular
staircases that faced in opposite directions.
They curved up to the second floor mezzanine
in graceful white marble covered with lush
crimson carpet. Opulence whispered its way
through the entire hotel. As Dannee glanced
up she noticed that the entire building was

hollow in the center, all the way to the roof. A balcony looked down on the lobby, with large hanging pots of greenery reaching to the floor below. The entire setting was cool and peaceful.

Over to the far right, Dannee could see a small bridge over a smaller stream which wound its way to a thatched roofed bar attached to the lobby. Vacationers sat in low, padded wicker chairs and enjoyed the view of tropical gardens overlooking gurgling waterfalls and pools of clear water with small fish darting back and forth.

The bellboy followed closely behind her as she walked to the registration desk on the left. It was a long expanse of dark wood that curved around a corner; men and women worked both ends, each apparently with a distinct duty to perform. She suddenly wished she had bought new luggage for this trip. Hers looked so middle-class, with stickers from the Grand Canyon, one corner dented and a scrape on its side. Why couldn't it have read "Cannes," or "Monte Carlo"? Or better yet, look like those pieces over there? Three pieces of matching luggage stood in the center of the aisle, all expensive leather with no stickers, no dents, no scrapes. She tilted her nose in the air. Digusting luggage, someone probably bought it to intimidate people like her!

"I'm Dannee Hathaway; I have a reservation." Her hands were shaking as the well dressed man behind the counter pushed a form toward her, handing her a pen to fill in the allotted spaces before he turned away to look through a stack of slips on the lower counter.

"Oh, yes, Miss Hathaway. You are one of the winners from the Ideal Supermarkets, *sí*? Did you have a pleasant trip?"

"Very pleasant, thank you." She spoke quietly. Did he have to announce to the world that she had won this trip as a prize?

The card was filled out quickly and her key was handed to a bellboy. "Your room is number 546, Miss Hathaway. Just sign your name and room number to the dinner checks and they will be taken care of accordingly." He handed her a small packet of coupons. "These are a few of the extras you are entitled to: a cruise of Acapulco Bay, two free drinks in any of our bars or the discotheque." He smiled, but Dannee was too busy blushing to smile back. He had all but informed the guests lined up behind her that she had won a trip she could not possibly afford and she was sure everyone in line had been able to hear him make his announcement. She turned and took a step, not seeing the tall, dark-haired man next to her until it was too late. She stepped on something soft just as a groan issued from just above her head. Hands reached out and grasped her arms, almost lifting her away from a blurred form. It had happened so quickly that Dannee clung to the counter to keep her balance, staring at the dark-haired man with the grimace on his face. His eyes were closed at first, but when he opened them, they were angry, dark blue chips.

"It would be nice if women with lethal shoes would warn men of their intent. Perhaps then we could defend ourselves accordingly," he gritted through clenched teeth. He had beautifully tanned skin, but at the moment it showed a tinge of bright red on his cheekbones and white around his mouth. Fleetingly, Dannee noticed that it would have been a sensuous mouth if it hadn't been distorted with anger.

"If you had stayed in line instead of pushing next to me, you might not have had such an unfortunate experience," she stated calmly. Her chin lifted with a tilt her mother would have called determined and her brother always referred to as stubborn, but the man gave no notice. "If you'll let me go, I promise to stay out of your way in the future." She gave a pointed glance at his hand, still gripping her arm, and his gaze followed hers. He dropped his hand immediately, a look of surprise darting across his face. One of the guests in line held out a cane of dark polished wood and brass that he had apparently dropped, unnoticed by Dannee until that moment. A deep blush crept into her face; she had stepped on the man's injured foot!

"Some women should not be allowed on the streets, let alone to travel by themselves," he muttered angrily as he placed his weight on the cane.

"I'm so sorry!" she exclaimed, hardly hearing his comments. But he was not to be easily appeased.

"Sorry you're traveling alone or sorry you stepped on my foot?" he retorted caustically, his words erasing any sympathy Dannee had felt.

Up came her chin again, but this time her brown eyes were sparkling back into his blue ones. "Neither," she replied sweetly. "I'm sorry I couldn't have stepped on your other foot so the pair could have matched your lame head!"

She marched away quickly as the laughter of the other guests filled her ears. Her face was flushed with anger and embarrassment. What was the matter with her? She had never been so rude before? Her back straightened. After all, he deserved it. He had made a major case out of a small incident. Handsome as he was, he was still a rude and arrogant man!

Somewhere in her mind was the realization that he was wealthy, for in the few minutes she had confronted him she had taken in the well tailored dark blue trousers, his light-weight pale blue pullover, and his shoes, which were definitely Italian leather. She had noticed that as she had stepped on one! Too bad he was such a contemptuous man; with his looks he should have been charming, the type of man one dreamed of meeting in an idyllic setting such as this.

She only wished she had not made such a scene. She should have said "excuse me" politely and beaten a hasty retreat. No. She should have—forget it, she told herself, as the bellboy led the way down the wide white-tiled hall toward her room. There was nothing she could do but stay out of that man's way. Perhaps he was only here for a day or two, though she doubted it. No one could come to such a paradise for just one or two days.

The room was perfect. It was decorated in shades of blues and greens with stark white walls, all restful and cheery. At an angle across one corner hung a blue-green patterned drape that matched the bedspread, and the carpeting picked up the same vibrant blue that was featured throughout the small suite. The bellboy unloaded her luggage as she peeked into the large spotless bathroom, also tiled in blue and green with the accessories in stark white.

As she turned back to the bedroom the bellboy was opening the drape to the balcony, revealing the most breathtaking view Dannee had ever seen. The blue Pacific stretched to the horizon, the slow moving waves tipped with small whitecaps here and there, which disappeared only to surface on the next wave. The water lapped at sand that was pure, white and fine. Large, swaying palm trees dotted the beach, the only protection from the hot, tropical sun that beat down on the more daring guests as they lay stretched out to welcome the heated rays like worshippers of an ancient god.

"Ohhh," Dannee sighed as she moved out to the railing. Then she noticed the large concrete window box in the corner, dripping bougainvillaea in bloom to cascade over the railing and down as far as the balcony below. Two white outdoor chairs and a small round table were in the other corner, making a perfect setting for morning coffee.

She heard a discreet cough from behind her and turned quickly. She had forgotten the young man who had so nicely, but quietly, looked after her needs. Apologizing quickly, she reached inside her purse, then handed him, in pesos, the tip he had obviously been expecting. He stared at it in amazement, then a smile covered his face.

"*Gracias, señorita.* If all is not well, please call for me and I will try to make it right. My name is Manuel."

"Thank you, Manuel." She smiled, too happy to worry about over-tipping. She had the rest of the week at her disposal and would learn what was expected by then.

He left quietly and she turned back to survey the scene from the balcony, its beauty more entrancing than anything she had ever seen. How was she going to leave this Eden when the time came? Was it possible to be filled with so much beauty that you became sated? She certainly didn't think so.

Later that afternoon, after unpacking and taking a refreshing shower, Dannee changed into a light yellow sundress and matching sandals. She might as well have a drink in the bar downstairs off the lobby while she looked through her guidebooks. Her eyes had been drawn to the mini-paradise when she had registered, and since it was too late to really sightsee, people-watching would be the next best thing.

She made her way down the hall toward the elevators, admiring the open balconies looking out toward the same scene as her room, each view giving a different perspective of the translucent blue water of the Pacific. She had never seen the ocean before and to a girl brought up surrounded by desert, it was quite an awe inspiring experience.

The thatched roofed bar off the lobby held only three or four customers and she gave a sigh of relief as she chose a chair next to the small pond that the bar was built over. It was nice not to be crowded and surrounded by rushing people.

The bartender took her order and returned quickly with a wide, salt-rimmed glass filled with a slushy marguerita, the most Mexican drink she could think of. It was fun ordering a drink in the middle of the afternoon and signing a check instead of paying cash; it seemed so worldly and was certainly different from what she did at home!

She watched the fish in the pond as they darted back and forth searching for the late afternoon shade of the ferns on the other side. They were as colorful as any Dannee had ever seen; even the goldfish were larger and brighter here. She leaned back and sighed in contentment.

The trip had actually been for two and her

best friend and co-worker at the insurance company, Norma, was supposed to have traveled with her. But at the last minute, she had come down with the flu and there wasn't enough time to find someone she would want to share the trip with, so she had come alone. It was a wonderful experience, but right now, Dannee wished there could have been someone else to talk to and share her experiences with. A constant, soft breeze ruffled her dark brown hair and she leaned back in her chair, closing her eyes. The wind caressed her skin gently; nature's air conditioning.

"So this is how the other half lives," she murmured to herself, and before she could take a sip of her drink, she had her answer.

"It depends on which other half you're talking about," came the cynical reply from behind her chair.

She turned quickly, almost spilling her drink in the process. Directly behind her, with his seat back touching hers, was the impossible man from the lobby! Her large brown eyes opened wide for just a second before she lowered thick, sooty lashes, giving him what she hoped was a coolly appraising look. He was doing the same, but there was a small smile tugging at the corner of his mouth.

"I beg your pardon?" she retorted in her iciest voice, hoping he would be properly chastised for speaking to her after the fiasco at the registration desk. He wasn't. She couldn't believe it, but it seemed that he was openly laughing at her!

"Don't tell me you're still mad at yourself for stepping on my foot?" One eyebrow was raised quizzically, just a hint of mockery in his voice. "Don't give it another thought. I've already accepted your apology."

"My apology?" she echoed, before truly understanding him. "*My* apology! I wouldn't apologize to you in a hundred years! Your behavior was rude, crude, and socially unacceptable! As far as I'm concerned Mr.—," She hesitated just a moment, not knowing his name, and he inserted it calmly for her.

"Cameron. Travis Cameron."

She continued, "Mr. Cameron, you can take a flying leap!"

She stood, hooking her purse in her arm and bending back over the table to retrieve her brochures with one hand and her drink with the other. She was definitely not going to sit next to him! She took a step back at the same time as she realized that his foot was in the narrow aisle. She tried to move her heel forward so she could avoid another accident, but instead lost her balance and landed ignobly in his lap, her slushy drink running slowly down his shirt front toward his expensive leather belt. His arms had gone around her automatically to hold her before she could slip to the ground in a heap, and for just a second they both watched the drink make a slow path down his chest, their faces matched in stunned surprise. His expression quickly changed, looking more like a thunderstorm as his flinty blue eyes locked with hers.

"Oh, I'm so sorry!" she exclaimed, trying to catch the slush with the rim of her glass, only succeeding in rubbing the cold liquid into his silk shirt.

"As soon as you get off my lap, I can quit playing Santa Claus, and get this mess cleaned up," he grated.

She hopped up quickly, more embarrassed than ever at her clumsiness, and feeling an overwhelming need to blame him for her lack of control. "If you hadn't been so rude, none of this would have happened!" she retorted angrily.

A waiter stood behind them, ready to clean up the mess and preclude any chance of further argument. Travis stood and took the cloth out of the man's hands to wipe his shirt dry, his eyes shooting angry messages at Dannee.

A light, musical, and definitely feminine laugh made them both turn around to face one of the most beautiful women Dannee had ever seen.

"Travis, I've always said your heart was cold, I just didn't know that the chill extended to other parts of your anatomy as well!" She smiled, her long, blond hair moving softly as she shook her head in disbelief. She was at least three inches taller than Dannee and had the chiseled features of a movie star, perfect in every detail, from her big, gray-shadowed eyes to her scarlet fingertips.

"It just so happens that this girl is a walking time bomb—working for the other side!"

Travis muttered, throwing down the towel. "Come to the room with me while I change, Miranda. If I don't get away from her quickly, I'm afraid I might say something I ought to regret—but won't!" He took the woman's arm and led her out of the bar, across the small bridge and toward the elevator, anger evident in every movement of his tapping cane. Miranda's voice rippled with laughter as the sounds, but not the words, of their conversation drifted to Dannee, filling her with another wave of embarrassment and something very much like an ache.

She smiled sheepishly at the waiter and sat down at another table. If nothing else, this vacation had started off with a bang!

Chapter Two

The lonely evening stretched ahead, settling depressively on Dannee's shoulders. She showered and changed her clothes, choosing an ankle length halter dress in shades of rust and chocolate with small gold hoop earrings that caught the light as she moved her head. As she clipped them to her ears, she wondered just what she would do to wile away the time until bed. She finally decided to spend some time in the lobby, went downstairs and wandered to one of the comfortable club chairs, to watch people passing through.

After having been embarrassed twice that day, and without Norma here to talk to, Dannee felt very awkward and very much alone. What does a single girl do on her own in a couple's resort? Certainly it was proper to wander around the hotel and visit the night entertainment it offered, but what about tomorrow? Was she doomed to spend her vacation on the hotel grounds? Suddenly she knew what the term "lonely in a crowd" meant, and silently commiserated with anyone who had ever been in this situation. Outwardly unconcerned, she watched young people, people her age, wandering through the plush entranceway. They were all paired off. Perhaps, when she had dinner, the waiter would place her at a table with others who were also alone. She lacked the nerve to ask, could only hope that her prayers would be answered.

With her mind made up, Dannee asked the desk captain for directions to the restaurant listed in her coupon book, then, following the small, winding path, was once again enchanted by the lush greenery. She heard the low rumbling of rushing water, and realized that the stream by the bar twisted around the exterior of the hotel grounds. She stopped, taking in the beauty of the ten foot waterfall gushing over strategically placed boulders and hardy, green ferns. At the base of the falls, crossing the pool of clear, blue water, was a rope and wood slatted suspension bridge, wide enough for two to walk side by side. Even now, there was a couple standing in the middle, watching the water flow into the pool below. It was twilight, and the girl's blond hair gleamed like bright moonbeams against the black sophistication of her long dress. The man beside her was wearing a dark tuxedo, but their faces were too far away and at such an angle that she couldn't see them. They epitomized the aura of romance Dannee felt the hotel possessed, completing the picture perfect look. That's what romance should be like, she thought to herself, sharing, talking, loving. . . .

Then she saw the cane leaning against the side of the bridge, and realized who was standing there with the beautiful woman. Her heart gave a surprising tug as she started to turn, but it was too late. He had spotted her staring and, with a mocking smile on his lips, he gave a small salute.

She walked away with her back ramrod straight. As she made her way down the path toward the restaurant, she felt embarrassed, not only at being caught, but at having her embarrassment confirmed by the flush on her cheeks. Honestly! That man was impossible!

The hacienda style restaurant was not yet crowded, but Dannee knew it would be filled as soon as darkness descended. Holiday people would enjoy the twilight hours outside as much as possible, especially with the secluded garden hideaways which surrounded the hotel.

The interior lights were dim, and only the candlelight on each table softened the shadows that leaped and flickered on the walls. She was escorted to a table for two overlooking the patio and the ocean beyond. Her eyes quickly adjusted to the darkness and she glanced around, intrigued. A glance around the room convinced her of how lucky she was that dinner was included with the trip, for it would have been totally beyond her budget to spend what this meal would cost!

In the deep red and gold interior, waiters stood like genies, ready to grant wishes at the first request for their attention. The music was soft and slow and definitely Latin, and it teased the atmosphere with love songs. She stared out over the blue and white-capped ocean lapping lazily against the sand. The perfect place for a honeymoon . . .

The waiter brought Dannee a menu and, when he left, she quickly fumbled through her small purse for the coupon she needed. She scanned it rapidly under the candlelight, hoping it would tell her what she could order.

"You may choose any of our steaks or seafood dinners, *señorita*. You also receive a complimentary glass of wine with your meal, along with coffee and dessert. Would you care to order now?"

She returned the waiter's smile as she ordered the largest steak on the menu. After all, she might never have another opportunity to sample what the rich took for granted.

She had been so busy looking around that she almost failed to see the couple silhouetted in the doorway. Then, defying his injured foot to impede his ability to maneuver gracefully around obstacles, Travis Cameron held the arm of the beautiful Miranda as they followed the waiter to their table, directly across from

Dannee. All she had to do was raise her head and she could stare right into his steely blue eyes.

The fake! He probably used that beautiful brass and wood cane to gain sympathy! But she couldn't deny his good looks, secretly acknowledging that he didn't really need that slight limp to gain any woman's eye. His broad shoulders and slim hips were shown off to advantage in his perfectly tailored tuxedo, making the rented variety seem gauche by comparison.

His dark hair had overtones of red in the candlelight—and his lashes! They were almost girlish, she thought waspishly, but the eyes beneath them were definitely masculine. Her eyes focused on his hands as they propped his walking stick against the unoccupied chair. They were tanned, as she imagined the rest of his body to be, but his fingers were long and graceful. Almost an artist's hands, she thought. Hands that would paint beautiful women with vivid strokes or play the violin until the melody brought tears. . . .

Once again he looked up and caught her staring at him, and as before, his glance was mocking. One eyebrow rose in question, and she quickly bent her head, hoping to hide the blush that pinked her cheeks. What was the matter with her anyway? She had never behaved this way before, toward anyone! She was both antagonistic and fascinated, all the while feeling she was excited about something. Him? No! Certainly not!

She ate the rest of her meal quickly. Everything placed before her was hot, and probably delicious, but she couldn't really have said what it tasted like. She was too busy not looking at that impossible man.

Dannee gave the waiter her coupon, signed the check, and left quickly. But not before noticing that Mr. Travis Cameron had been busy all through dinner. Miranda had carried on a continuous, animated conversation, and had made him chuckle softly several times. A small stab of pain went through Dannee as the restaurant door closed silently behind her. Why should she cause only havoc when he was around? It didn't matter, she tried to tell herself briskly, as she walked along the moonlit path toward the sleepy-slow sound of waves on the beach. After all, he had been insulting to her since they first met! Why should she care if his attention was directed elsewhere?

The sea shimmered gray in the pale light of the moon. The waves seemed to move slowly, leisurely, lapping in slow motion at the iridescent shore. The rhythm was soothing, almost a lullaby to Dannee, as it methodically washed through her mind, relaxing unconsciously tensed nerves.

She sank to the sand, not far from where the smooth water was fanning lightly, methodically, at the shore. The warm grains still held the heat of the afternoon sun, and this too soothed Dannee. She curled her arms around her knees, suddenly tired from the events of the day.

This time last night, she had been in her parents' living room, showing them her new clothes, and trying to convince her brother that he would enjoy making the trip to Acapulco with her to see the sights. However, like all seventeen year old boys, traveling with his sister was tantamount to traveling with his parents—definitely "No Go!"

"Forget it, Dannee! I'd cramp your style and I know you'd cramp mine! What guy wants his sister looking over his shoulder when he tries to make headway with a beautiful *señorita*?" He had made a face, his dark hair falling over his forehead reminding her of when he was a small boy, all devil, very little angel! When he was younger, he was always in the middle of her dates, asking them the wrong questions, volunteering all the wrong answers and embarrassing her with facts that should never have been allowed out of the family closet. He was always into something; charging her boyfriends for bringing in cold drinks; charging them for *not* bringing in cold drinks.

She too had been much younger then. Everything was a life threatening crisis in those years, and her complaints could be heard for miles. She smiled, her thoughts still with her family as she turned over a small shell at her feet to see the glow of mother of pearl cupped inside.

He had turned out to be a much better brother than she ever would have guessed. He was almost six years younger than Dannee, but now felt it was his place to protect her, rather than to haunt her. They had actually had some good times together this past year. He was growing up.

When Dannee moved out of the house into an apartment with her best friend, Norma, it was a turning point in her relationship with her brother. They turned from instant enmity to cautious friends, strengthening a relationship that had been seeded years before, but needed separation to bring it to bloom. He was no longer hassled because she knew the small details of his life, and she no longer worried about his practical jokes with her dates. As the pressure was released, so was the sibling antagonism that accompanied it, and they developed a friendship as persons in their own right. Funny! she thought. We probably know more about each other's thoughts now than when we shared the same home!

"One day away from home, and I'm homesick," she muttered. "What's the matter with me?"

She stretched out on the sand. Her skin, bathed in the moonlight, glimmered with a soft, coppery glow. She didn't realize how much she resembled a goddess of the golden moon. Her dress was muted, her hair dark, and only her skin held a shining mother-of-pearl iridescence in the softened light. A cloud passed over the moon and she shivered. It was time to go to her room. A good night's rest was exactly what she needed.

She stood gracefully, ignoring the sand that clung to her skirt, and walked slowly back up

the path to the hotel. She didn't see the tall
stranger who stood on a darkened balcony five
floors up. His eyes followed her as she made
her way up the path, and he sipped his drink
as she slipped out of sight. Slowly, he walked
back into the dim room and silently closed the
sliding glass doors.

The morning light crept into the room,
slowly awakening Dannee with its warming
rays. For just a moment she forgot where she
was, and her sleepy eyes darted around the
room in confusion. They settled on the balcony outside and everything slipped into
place. This was Acapulco, land of the sun!
   Hopping out of bed, she almost skipped to
the large patio. This was the perfect morning
to have coffee on the terrace. The sun was
shining, the Pacific was just as blue as yesterday, and the agile, brown bodies of the small
children playing in the sand were as lovable
as she had first thought. All the stifling home-
sickness and depression of the night before
had miraculously lifted from her shoulders.
Today was going to be perfect!
   Dannee rang room service and gave her
order in clear but stilted Spanish, crossing her
fingers as she hung up the phone. She hoped
she had given the correct names for the food
she had ordered. She had the distinct feeling
that the girl who had taken her order was
laughing at her!
   She grabbed her clothing, a golden yellow
bathing suit and a long, white eyelet bathing

robe, and headed toward the shower. The warm water felt good beating down on her smooth back, waking her up even more than the sunshine. This had to be the most glorious part of all, waking with nothing to do but dress casually and enjoy the day stretching ahead. No work—no boss—no busy schedule—no cleaning, nothing to do but enjoy herself!

As she was putting the finishing touches on her makeup there was a knock on the door; the waiter had arrived with her breakfast. Quickly, she signed the check and gave him a tip and a warm smile, both of which he received with grace and a slight bow.

Nothing delighted Dannee more than drinking piping hot coffee and munching soft, warm rolls with butter and honey on her own balcony in the bright morning sun. She sat back and closed her eyes with a sigh of contentment. This was the perfect vacation. Thank heaven for Ideal Supermarkets! If the owner were around, Dannee felt she could have kissed him for having such a marvelous prize for his contest. Thank heaven she won! It had been a long time since she had been able to relax and enjoy the freedom of just being alive!

She searched through her purse, looking for the coupon book provided by the hotel. There was a coupon good for one cruise of Acapulco Bay at sunset. It sounded so lovely, so romantic, she wished once more that she had someone with whom to share the experience. Mentally, she shook herself. It was just as well, for if there were a man present, she just might succumb to the delights of love, and that was something she was *not* ready for. It would be years before she would settle down and raise the family everyone else seemed to desire; everyone except herself. She was going to have money in the bank, a good career, be self-sufficient. All her friends could think of nothing but their boyfriends and turning them into husbands; but Dannee thought that was just slightly short of stupid. Who wanted someone to boss them around just when they had earned the ability to be their own bosses? She sniffed. Only the weak, she told herself.

She glanced down, surprised to find the coupon still in her hand. She stared at it, but saw instead the face of a man with dark hair that curled at the ends to slightly overlap his collar; bright blue eyes that turned ice cold gray to warm, Pacific blue. She shook her head. This was madness! She was better off never seeing the man again when his mere presence rendered her gauche and ungraceful!

Dannee received directions to the pool from one of the small, spritely maids in the large foyer outside her room. She made her way downstairs and out to the twisting path winding through more of the carefully kept tropical gardens. She stopped occasionally, people-watching, as usual, and almost collided with more than one guest. They were all dressed as she was, bathing suits, sandals and robes slung over arms or shoulders. It was a genial atmosphere. Almost everyone had a smile and nod for the preoccupied young girl, so apparently awed by her surroundings. When she reached the largest of the hotel's five pools, she stopped, stunned by the scene in front of her. It had to be a mirage! The pool was large, shaped like a four-leaf clover, but at one end was a tall, well-placed rocky cliff over which streamed another full, flowing waterfall. A few of the guests were lying on air-mattresses, tanning their bodies and letting the water gently rock them to sleep, while others swam or sat talking in groups on the comfortable lounge chairs situated by the edge of the pool. Still others walked under the falls to return with drinks in their hands and happy grins on their faces. Dannee bent down, squinting to see what was behind the veil of water. She could see the outline of a bar, with stools apparently set underwater, and bartenders serving drinks to those who dared to enter.

"Unusual, isn't it?" A low voice spoke behind her.

She turned, with the dreaded feeling of once again meeting the devil of her thoughts. Her eyes widened involuntarily. He was clad in skintight black bathing trunks that seemed molded to his lean hips, accentuating his broad, tanned chest and taut thighs. Her eyes sought the line where his bathing suit met his hips in an effort to see if his skin was lighter in color when kept from the sun.

"Yes, I'm tanned all over." His voice held an undercurrent of laughter, just enough to make her uncomfortable at being so easy to read, but not enough to anger her.

"Narcissism fits the overall picture, somehow," she proclaimed primly, as she turned and began walking away. A hand on her arm arrested her flight.

She heard his sigh of exasperation, but could not look at his face to confirm it. Her eyes were riveted to the dark, curly hair on his chest.

"Do you think of things to do and say in the dark of night just to get back at me for some imagined injustice?"

"Of course not!"

"Then can't we bury the hatchet somewhere besides my chest? If I apologize for whatever it is you hold against me, can we then be friends?"

"No. And no again, Mr. Cameron," she stated, looking pointedly at his hand on her arm. "And now, if you don't mind, I'd like to swim."

Turning, she stalked off, knowing intuitively that angering him was her only protection, but not quite certain why it was so important to protect herself from him. She didn't want to think about it, but the words "self preservation" kept crowding into her thoughts. . . .

Chapter Three

Dannee leafed through the brochure once more as she attempted to choose which tour to take. The one to Coyuca Lagoon sounded fascinating, and she tried to envision flamingos and pelicans surrounding the swimmers in the freshwater lagoon; but another tour announced the fact that if one had never been to Acapulco, *this* was the tour to take. It would acquaint one with the city and public beaches, ending with the high-divers off the cliffs of Acapulco into the swirling ocean below.

"For a small tourist town, it has a lot to offer." A deep, male voice broke into her musings and she stiffened, knowing immediately to whom the voice belonged. He stood looking down at her, his dark hair curling, slightly damp. His blue eyes twinkled as he watched her mentally deciding whether to be nice or rude. He smiled as she reached her decision.

"Yes, it is unusual, isn't it?" She answered sweetly, contradicting the sparkle of anger in her eyes. Why wouldn't this man leave her alone? Didn't he have enough beautiful women falling all over him? Did he enjoy watching her play the fool whenever he was around? Did he want to see what other tricks he could make her perform in her nervousness? "You must enjoy it very much. It's a virtual playground for playboys," she said.

He grinned even more widely and it dimpled one cheek. "Are you implying I'm a playboy, Miss Hathaway?"

Her cheeks reddened lightly. That *was* what she had meant, but she certainly hadn't thought he would be rude enough to point it out!

"If the implication fits, Mr. Cameron?" she answered, before turning her attention to the brochure in her hand. She pretended to read, but could not really see the bold print.

"If I'm the one to decide, then I say no." His voice shook a little, probably with laughter, but she wouldn't look up, wouldn't give him the satisfaction of allowing him to know just how much he disturbed her. Out of the corner of her eye she could see him shift his weight before he sat down in the chair next to her.

Not knowing what else to do, she ignored him, continuing to stare at the brochure.

"Do you read *that* slowly, or does my presence bother you?"

"Neither, Mr. Cameron," she retorted breezily, eyes glued to the shiny paper as her mind whirled in confusion.

He sighed. "Travis. My name is Travis, and I will call you Dannee." He spoke with authority, the decision made. She nodded in acquiescence, bowing to his will. What would be the point in fighting his decision? She sensed already that she could never win against him if he really wanted something.

"Look, Dannee, I think we need to clear the air between us. We're obviously going to be running into each other for the duration of this vacation, so wouldn't it be wiser to be friends, instead of trying to treat each other with barely veiled animosity? Can't we begin again?"

Carefully, she placed the brochures in her lap and clasped her hands together slowly and deliberately, trying not to clench them. For some reason, she didn't want to delve into this. He stirred her emotions, and caused her to react strangely.

"Do you mean you want to go through that whole lobby scene again? My stepping on your foot? Your rudeness?" she questioned sweetly, deliberately misunderstanding. She didn't know why, but something told her to steer clear of this man.

"I mean to begin again. This time *without* my rudeness and *without* your clumsiness." He waved his hand, dismissing the warlike gleam in her eyes. "I'm sorry, I didn't mean it the way it sounded. I really want to become friends."

"Why?"

"Does there have to be a reason?" he asked in exasperation.

He apparently decided to take another tack. "I want to be friends because I don't like enemies, Dannee. In my business, most associates are competitors, and competitors are enemies. I have enough of those."

"All right, Mr. Cameron, we'll begin again," she stated primly, her back ramrod straight as the stared at the hands in her lap. Were they hers? And if so, why were they trembling?

"Thank you, Dannee," he murmured, sitting back in his seat and pulling out a gold filigree cigarette case. "And how are you enjoying Acapulco so far?"

"Oh, I love it. Everything is so beautiful and even more exciting than I imagined. This is a tropical paradise just made for lovers."

His brow rose in question and she stammered, "I mean—for people. It seems as if everyone is in twos, that's all," she muttered, once again embarrassed. Why couldn't she put words together coherently around this man? She wasn't this way at home, or anywhere else for that matter!

His voice was soft, understanding, as he questioned her. "And is it just a little lonely in 'ones,' Dannee?"

"Well, it's different. As I'm sure you overheard at the registration desk yesterday, I won this trip. But it was a trip for two, and my roommate was going to accompany me; however, the flu struck and I had to come alone."

"Male or female?"

"Pardon?"

"Your roommate," he persisted. "Is your roommate male or female?"

"Does it matter, Mr. Cameron?" she retorted haughtily. "I should think that would be my own affair."

"Female." He pronounced with satisfaction, and her brown eyes shot sparks at his accuracy.

But she was unwilling to confirm his statement, and so she hedged. "Why do you say that? Is it so unlikely that I would attract a man?"

"Not unlikely at all," he answered smoothly. "But a girl who lives with a man usually has no qualms about admitting it. In fact, it may increase her sex appeal to others. If one man wants her enough to live with her then obviously she has something other men might want."

She glanced up at him and saw the gentle sparkle of laughter in his eyes. She couldn't help it, she began chuckling, laughter bubbling in her throat. "You're right, of course,"

41

she finally answered. "My roommate's name is Norma, and I miss her. As I said before, this seems to be a vacation spot built for twos."

"I don't know about being built for twos, but it certainly wasn't made for slaving away at a typewriter." A low, lilting voice spoke from behind Dannee.

She knew the voice; it belonged to the beautiful woman Travis called Miranda. Would Miranda be irritated to find her here with her boyfriend? The other woman moved with lithe grace around the couch and chose a large, curved chair across from them, molding her tall, well-formed body to its upholstered curves.

Dannee's heart plummeted in the face of Miranda's beauty. She felt like a moth next to a butterfly; they both had wings, and flew, but there the resemblance ended.

Miranda's voice broke into her thoughts. "Are you enjoying your vacation, Miss—?"

"Hathaway, Dannee Hathaway. Yes, I am, very much."

"So am I, Dannee." Miranda brushed her long, blond hair away from her face, exposing a long, slender throat.

Was there nothing wrong with this girl? Did she never get a rash? Had she never broken her longest nail?

"I almost hate to start work this morning. I'd love to be outside next to one of the pools getting a suntan to take back to Santa Fe with me." Her voice sounded wistful, but her words left Dannee confused.

Dannee's brow furrowed as she glanced from Miranda to Travis. "Work? I thought you were here on vacation."

"Goodness, no! I'm Travis's secretary. Didn't he tell you?" She shook her head at the tall, lean man with a smile. "He has business here, and I was needed. I'm just a poor secretary whose only bonus in life is a boss who travels a lot." She grinned. "Come to think of it, that's not so bad!"

"And you're not so poor, either, if I recall your last raise in salary correctly," Travis muttered in mock disgust.

Dannee giggled, her spirits suddenly buoyant again. She didn't want to examine why and pushed all her questions to the back of her mind, to be answered later, when she was alone with her thoughts. "That sounds like the job every secretary dreams of! How lucky! Do you really travel so much?"

"Oh, yes. We just came back from Tahoe, where Travis closed a deal before we could devote ourselves to skiing. That's how he broke his foot." Miranda glanced at Travis, a twinkle in her eye. "He broke a small bone, you see, but they can't put it in a cast, so he has to rest it and use a cane for a few weeks. It seems to be working out well, though. Now he has a weapon with which to fight off the women."

Just as she finished speaking, a young girl who Dannee guessed to be around nineteen, walked past, smiling a welcome to Travis. He pointedly ignored her, a frown creasing his

43

brow as he contemplated the ground. "What is this, Miranda. Pick on your boss week?" he muttered, shifting uncomfortably.

"Why, Mr. Cameron. You know I have only good things to say about you!" she said teasingly, her eyes wide and innocent and her voice even more so.

They all laughed. When the waiter came around, they ordered coffee and continued the conversation. They were fun to talk to and Dannee found she had lost the loneliness that had seemed to dog her heels so relentlessly for the past day.

In a teasing, bantering tone, Miranda and Dannee discussed the idiosyncrasies of bosses, describing their total inability to communicate with anyone other than a dictating machine; how most expected their secretary's complete devotion to a job that paid by the week or the month, rather than by the hours of seemingly necessary overtime.

"Come on!" Travis groaned. "You women aren't so perfect either! How many times do I walk down the halls to find the typists freshening their makeup, while the file clerks file nothing but their nails?"

He was so relaxed, his blue eyes warm and merry, that Dannee felt her throat constrict with the feelings his look sent through her. Gone was the arrogance, the coldness she had been exposed to on their first meeting. When he wished to charm, he could do it with the expertise of an Indian with his cobra!

"Ah, *Señor* Cameron. I was looking for you earlier." An older man stopped by Travis's chair. "I want to discuss that new chain with you; I need a few more details."

Travis stood, a mask covering his face as he shook hands, then led the gentleman away without the usual introductions. Dannee was suddenly deflated. Perhaps he hadn't wanted the man to know he had no one to talk to except a lonely nobody in the lobby. Perhaps he was even using the man as an excuse to leave Dannee's company.

Miranda seemed to guess the emotions Dannee was fighting. She smiled, placing her hand over Dannee's. "Business is always so hard to separate from personal life, but Travis tries. He's down here for two reasons and both are related to business, so he gets very little time to relax."

"I'm sure," Dannee muttered, as she gathered her brochures together and reached for her handbag. "But if I'm going to see something of Acapulco, I'd better get going. It was nice meeting you, Miranda. I hope I see you again before I leave." She meant what she said. The past hour had flown, and Miranda had proved to be as nice to talk to as she was beautiful. Darn it!

"Why don't you join Miranda and me for a drink this afternoon?" Travis's voice came suddenly from behind her and she turned, startled, only to lose her footing and fall into his arms—again!

He grasped her waist and held her upright until she steadied herself. His hands loosened their hold, but didn't give it up, almost caressing her waist as their eyes met and held. The world stopped turning for what seemed like hours. She forgot why he was holding her, or how she had arrived there. All she was aware of was the warm, funny feeling that invaded her limbs and made her answer his slow, easy smile with one of her own.

"Goodness! Are you all right, Dannee?" Miranda broke the spell, bringing Dannee down to earth, leaving her shattered and embarrassed.

Travis's eyes glinted with mischief. "It seems that either I rattle Dannee or she needs a bodyguard to protect her from herself."

Dannee pulled her hands away from his chest and turned away from him, her face flaming. "It seems you're extremely unlucky for me to be around, Mr. Cameron. I'd better stay away from you if I want to stay in one piece!"

"Either that, or I'm your guardian angel. When next we meet, say at three-thirty at the main bar, I'll stay on the opposite side of the table," he said softly. "I think I enjoy your company, even if you try not to enjoy mine."

"Think? If you don't know, then don't expect me to give you a repeat performance. You've had your chance and you blew it," she stated emphatically, giving away more of herself than she realized.

"I haven't had my chance, *yet!* But I will."

She turned and walked away swiftly, clutching her purse. She could hear Miranda's voice calling to her. "See you at three-thirty, Dannee!"

Chapter Four

The time she had spent in the lobby with
Miranda and Travis had slipped by so quickly
that, in the end, Dannee missed most of the
tour groups. She quickly decided to pursue
one of the tans that everyone else carried
like banners of a vacation lazily spent wor-
shipping a tropical sun. It was another clear
day with little puffs of clouds sitting like
cotton balls on an invisible table in the sky.
She quickly changed into her swimsuit and
slipped into a pair of jeans and T-shirt so she
could walk to the beach. She didn't feel quite
comfortable walking through the crowded
hotel and grounds in her bikini.

She strolled along the beach, the fine white
sand already warm under her feet, and she

could imagine how hot it would be this afternoon. The flags were up to warn swimmers of the strong undertow, yet the sea looked so calm and serene. She splashed at the water's edge and felt the grip of the undertow, amazed that it could be so deceiving.

Travis was deceiving, too. He had been arrogant and cold when she first met him, a human iceberg. But since then, just this morning in the lobby, for instance, he had shown another side of himself, a warm, funny side that she didn't think many others got to see, and she wondered why he had allowed her to glimpse what must be a very private part of his nature. It must be lonely, being a successful businessman, and a single one at that. Not only would business problems have to be coped with, but social problems would have to be dealt with, too. Obligations and self-reliance went hand in hand, but that didn't alter the fact that he must get lonely sometimes, too.

She smiled. Her dad was a quoter of cliches and this would probably call for, "it's lonely at the top" or "money can't buy happiness." Her smile widened. She could almost see him spouting his quotes, then raising his eyebrows, glancing over the rims of his bifocals, waiting for the profound truth of his words to sink into his listener's head.

Her thoughts turned once again to Travis. What sort of business was he in? Neither Miranda nor Travis had said, and she had forgotten to ask. She shrugged her shoulders and kicked a small shell. She would ask the next time they met. This afternoon, if she could face him again.

Why did she always seem to trip or drop things when he was within her sphere? For the past twenty-two years she had been known to be generally witty, pretty and optimistic. But never—never—had she been known to be clumsy!

"*Señorita! Señorita!* You want to ride? I have a beautiful horse. You want to ride on the beach?" The small, dark-skinned boy ran beside her, a thin hand holding onto his sombrero as he tried to keep pace with her steps. "Only five dollars, *señorita,* and you can ride along the beach on a golden stallion, just like in the movies!"

Dannee slowed her pace, smiling at the pleading expression on the boy's face. He was dressed in denim cutoffs and a large, straw sombrero with a shabby brim that lifted in the wind and, along with his dusky eyes, gave the impression of a forlorn, but hopeful imp.

"See my beautiful horse, *señorita*?" He waved his hand toward a thatched roof on stilts, where several horses were corraled while other tourists picked and chose. "Mine is the best!"

He grabbed her hand and she allowed him to lead her into the shadow of the roof, grinning at his enthusiasm. Why not take a ride along the beach? Indeed, wasn't that what postcards were made of?

"This is a golden stallion?" she asked incredulously, a few minutes later, pointing to a brown, swaybacked horse with its head drooping in the heat of the sun.

"Well . . ." he murmured, "It is a stallion, no?"

"No," she said emphatically.

His face dropped.

"But, I'll rent it anyway," she said with a smile.

A grin exploded on his small face as he led the horse out of the enclosure into the bright sunlight. "Do you wish to go alone or with a group, *señorita*? One is starting up right now."

"I'll go alone, and thank you for the use of your fine horse."

The boy pulled at her sleeve as she slipped her foot into the stirrup. "Five dollars, *señorita*, please."

"I should have known, a businessman at heart. Pay in advance," she muttered as she pulled the money from her back pocket.

Within minutes, the business end of the transaction had taken place, directions had been given, and Dannee was on the horse's back trotting down the beach toward the curve of the cove. Despite the "stallion's" looks, it was strong, and seemed durable. Its legs were sturdy and its gaits more comfortable than the swayback had promised.

Dannee reveled in the blue sky and even bluer water, and gave the horse a nudge to move it into an easy canter. A soft breeze ruffled her hair, cooling her neck and shoulders, making her feel close to the wonders nature had so abundantly provided. The beach was deserted and she could almost imagine this land as the first Spaniards must have found it: wild, untamed, breathtakingly beautiful. Mountains rose to her left, tall, covered with jungle growth as far as the eye could see. She pulled gently on the reins, slowing the horse to a walk, then stopping him completely as she neared a small grove of trees sheltering a lagoon of crystal clear water.

Brightly feathered birds of every description flew about, diving, swooping to the water's surface before hearing her approach, then soaring high into the cloud-vaulted sky. This had to be a freshwater lagoon for so many of the birds to rest here. She slid off the horse and glanced down the beach, noticing that she couldn't be more than four or five hundred yards from the edge of the sea at high tide, yet here was a small piece of Eden. Quickly, she tied the reins to a bush, stripped off her clothes to the bathing suit beneath, glancing over her shoulder to assure herself that no one was watching. Then she dived, allowing the water to fold her into its depths, welcoming its coolness on her heated skin. It was glorious! She surfaced and stroked across to the other bank, then back again, reveling in the feeling of being the only person in Paradise. It would have been nice though, if there had been an Adam to play with Eve—or a Travis to play with Dannee. No! She shook the water from her face and trod water. Those were dangerous thoughts; better to think of something else than to dream of what she could never have.

The swaybacked "stallion" whinnied and Dannee looked up, but spotted nothing alarming. Probably one of the birds had spooked him. She heard the soft thud of hooves, but reason told her it was just a group of riders who had left behind her. The sounds faded and she knew she had been foolish for hoping it had been Travis. He was no doubt busy elsewhere, with business—or pleasure.

She floated on her back to the spot on the bank where she had started and reluctantly pulled herself onto the sand, lying in the sun to dry off before she donned her jeans and shirt. It was time to rejoin civilization. Somehow, it was all too wonderful to absorb. She opened her eyes and gazed at the sky. Wouldn't it be nice to share this with someone? Someone with sparkling eyes as blue as the sky? Someone with dark, springy hair that curled around his neck and ached to be touched?

She stood quickly, and dusted sand from her legs and arms with short, angry movements. *Stop it!* That someone has other interests; judging from the warm gleam in his eyes when he looks at Miranda, he's already taken. And by a very nice person, too. Don't be a spoilsport, Dannee, she told herself angrily.

Besides, she asked herself dejectedly, with Miranda around, why would he prefer you?

She never thought to ask herself why she should be so interested in Travis when she had scorned any romantic thoughts for so long.

Back in her room, a cool, refreshing shower washed the sand from her body and tangled hair. She stepped into a peach halter dress and white sandals before drying her hair with a blower, curling it softly to frame her face and hang to her shoulders in thick, dark waves. Her makeup was light, she didn't need much because of the amount of sun she had already absorbed. Her skin had turned a golden toast color, more becoming than she realized. One glance in the mirror told her she looked good with her shining brown hair, wide, brown eyes and peach-tinted lips.

It was almost three-thirty as she wound her way through the groups of tourists heading toward the bar. Her heart was beating fast, but she determinedly told herself that it had been the exhilarating ride and the rush to dress that made her feel this way. But she knew her lie for what it was the moment she caught Travis's eyes on her. He sat alone with Miranda in the curve of the bar overlooking the stream; large pineapples containing some tropical concoction sat on the small table between them. But Dannee barely noticed any of that as her eyes locked with Travis's. Everything else went out of focus as she read his admiring glance, and a smile tugged at her mouth, while a blush tinged her cheeks.

They were alone, the only two people in the world. She continued to weave through the tables, smiling, before she realized that she had forgotten Miranda, who was probably watching her make a darn fool of herself!

"Is this a mutual admiration society for two, or can anyone join in?" Miranda's voice broke Travis's gaze and his eyes abruptly reverted to the blonde.

Somehow, Dannee knew Miranda's smile was not genuine and she felt saddened, plummeting quickly back to earth. In a few days she would leave and Travis would be with Miranda again. This feeling that seemed to affect them both so strongly was just chemistry, not some kind of love at first sight. Keep it in perspective, Dannee, she warned herself.

She slipped into the seat across from them, knowing her knees would collapse soon if she didn't. "Oh, this is for anyone who loves Acapulco! People act differently here than they would at home; but they recover their senses when they leave. So goes common sense on vacations!"

Miranda's laughter tinkled through the air, but Dannee was surprised at Travis's frown. "You think most people go away for a holiday and invite things to happen that they wouldn't want to happen at home?" he questioned.

"Of course," Dannee stated airily, ignoring the tight band suddenly constricting her ribs and interfering with her regular breathing pattern. "Don't you? I mean, shipboard romances and Acapulco courtships have a lot in common, wouldn't you say?"

"Of course. Any seasoned traveler, such as yourself, knows that," Travis muttered, frowning at a small chunk of pineapple bobbing in his drink.

"Don't choke on that, Travis," Miranda murmured, a twinkle in her eye, as if she knew exactly what he was thinking. He sent her a quelling glance before looking back at Dannee. "And what did you do this morning?" he asked conversationally, his smile stiff.

"It was too late to take a tour, so I rented a horse and rode along the beach.

"You know how to ride?" Miranda questioned.

"In El Paso everyone knows how to ride, or lies about it." Dannee laughed. "But I really do ride. My dad runs a small ranch outside of town."

She tried to ignore the thudding of her heart as Travis watched her closely over the rim of his drink. He seemed so relaxed as he leaned back in his chair and watched her through hooded eyes; but she knew he was paying close attention to the conversation, and wondered what he was thinking that was making him frown so gloomily.

"I found this lovely lagoon and took a quick swim. It could have been out of a movie set."

"It probably was. Didn't you know this is where the old Tarzan movies were filmed?" Travis drawled. His frown disappeared, only to be replaced by a cool, dissecting appraisal that made her nerve ends tingle.

"No, I didn't know that," she answered. "But I know a young man who will be very sorry he missed this trip. He was a great fan of Tarzan movies. He even broke his arm when he tried to swing from one mesquite tree to another and missed his target!" Dannee chuckled, remembering her brother's antics.

"Oh? A childhood boyfriend?"

"My brother." She saw his satisfied smile too late to stop her flow of words. Darn! She should have played coy and let him think it *was* a boyfriend! Why couldn't she keep her mouth shut? However, the thought of any of the boys she knew swinging from trees quickly brought back her sense of humor.

"And why didn't he join you?"

"One reason he gave was that he didn't want me looking over his shoulder while he invited a pretty *señorita* to look at his postcard collection." Dannee grinned. "But the main reason was his job. He starts college next year and needs the money; besides, he likes what he does. He wants to be a golf course architect, of all things, and he's working as a gardener for a wealthy gentleman of ill-repute. He couldn't see giving up a week's salary for a five day vacation." She brushed an errant curl away from her cheek just as the silent bartender placed a large pineapple drink in front of her. Her eyebrows rose in a silent question, but she received no answer.

She supposed that Travis had already ordered for her; taking over seemed to come naturally to him.

"You sound as if you're not too thrilled with his employer." Travis looked intently at her as he asked his question.

"I'm not. He's forty-five years old and he's been married three times. He thinks the way to his money is through his bedroom and I don't think that's a good example for any young man to follow."

"You don't think all rich men are like that, do you?"

Dannee nodded. "I think most of them are. They believe all they have to do is wave a few bills under a girl's nose and they can get whatever they want."

"Everyone has a price."

"Granted. But the price may not be money. It may be love, or peace, or contentment, or any number of things. Money is only one commodity. I think most wealthy people forget that fact."

Suddenly her eyes widened. She realized that a man who travelled everywhere with his secretary must be very rich, so she had just accused Travis Cameron of being in the same class as the wealthy "gentleman of ill-repute" she'd just mentioned. "Present company excluded," she muttered hastily.

There was a moment of stunned silence before both Miranda and Travis burst into laughter. Darn them! Did they have to make her feel like the court jester? In all fairness, though, she had left herself wide open for teasing when she had spoken her views without thinking, and after seeing the sunny side of it, she began laughing, too.

Miranda wiped her eyes with the corner of a napkin. "I must say, Dannee, you are the most refreshing girl I've met in a long time! Most of the women I meet are so worldly and jaded, they're boring. All of them are out selling what you just accused rich men of buying."

"Just remember, Dannee, no one can buy what isn't for sale," Travis said, but the laughter was still in his eyes and a smile softened his lips.

"Maybe so, but wealth isn't everything," she said primly, before mischief sparkled in her eyes. "However, I do admit that it's nice to win contests from rich supermarket owners and be treated like royalty for a little while. I may even change my opinion and decide I don't want to go back to poverty when this is over!" She sipped her drink, hearing and ignoring Travis's chuckle. She missed the puzzled look that crossed Miranda's face and the imperceptible shake of her host's head.

"That reminds me, I understand there's going to be a cocktail party tomorrow night for the contest winners. You'll be going, won't you?" Travis casually smoothed the crease in his tan slacks, eyes focused on an invisible speck of lint.

"I don't know. I haven't heard anything about it."

"You'll probably receive the invitation in your box today. Miranda and I have been invited, and we'd like you to sit with us, wouldn't we, Miranda?"

Miranda nodded her head, looking slightly more reserved than usual, and Dannee wondered miserably if Miranda thought she was trying to edge in where she wasn't wanted. She genuinely liked the other woman and hoped they could be friends for the next five days.

"Thank you for the offer, but I think I'd better see how things go. I want to sign up for several tours. After all, I probably won't get to see Acapulco again for quite some time, so I'd better make the most of it while I have the chance."

"Nonsense! This is a party to celebrate your winning the contest, so in a sense, it's in your honor. There will be over twenty other couples invited for this, so you'll be well chaperoned."

"Over twenty other winners?" she repeated incredulously.

"The grocery chain has forty-seven stores and each store boasts a winner. The winners were split into two groups, with one group coming this week and one group next week," Miranda pointed out.

"I can't refuse, then, can I?"

The rest of the afternoon was spent in relaxing conversation on safer topics, with everyone enjoying the soft breeze and the muted tones of a guitar drifting from some where in the vicinity of the pool.

When it was time to go, Dannee knew without a doubt that she would have dinner in her room, sit curled up on her patio to watch the sunset, then call it a night. Her eyelids were already drooping from the unusual amount of exercise she had taken, not to mention the strain her nerves had been under from being in Travis Cameron's presence.

They said good-bye. She walked slowly to her room, stopping briefly at the desk to find the invitation in her box, just as Travis had promised. Again, she had forgotten to inquire about the nature of Travis's business. She shrugged her shoulders. It wasn't important anyway. She must stay away from Travis, and forget the closeness she sensed they could achieve in the short time they could have together. Miranda was in the picture, and Dannee was not the type to play siren, luring men to her.

A small sad smile etched her face as she stood in the elevator. Who was she kidding? Miranda was like a beautifully dressed, nineteenth-century doll; next to her, Dannee looked like a Kewpie doll—sweet—cute, but certainly not devastating enough to steal any-one's heart!

Chapter Five

Dannee did exactly what she'd planned to do. Room service brought a club sandwich and a tall cool concoction in a frosty glass right to her door. Seated on her balcony, she munched and watched the sunset put on a show only the most blasé could fail to exclaim over. The sky turned pale pink before showing its veils of violet and deep blue.

Soon after retiring to her room, she propped herself in bed with a historical romance set in the heart of Mexico. By the time she closed her eyes, the hero had turned into a dark, sophisticated man who just might have walked with a cane and the heroine bore a striking resemblance to herself.

By the time bright sunlight spilled across the carpet onto her bed, she had been carried off to a mountain retreat in her lover's arms. She awoke grinning in delight before she remembered that the hero in the book was blond, and that no one had volunteered to carry her anywhere. Her spirits drooped considerably when she realized the heroine had also been beautiful, like Miranda. Miranda! It would have been so much easier to feel right about her feelings for Travis if Miranda was a witch. But she wasn't. She was nice— and sweet—and offered the hand of friendship. How could Dannee contemplate hurting someone so kind, so charming?

Her spirits drooped even further. How could she dream of stealing someone like Travis when Miranda was around? No matter what *she* wanted to do, Travis would never be interested. Anyone in his right mind would choose Miranda over her. She had to be crazy to even think of such a thing! Travis was just being nice to a lonely girl, that was all. . . .

Dannee remembered stepping on his foot, then spilling her drink ignobly in his lap. What got into her when he was around? She groaned, remembering yesterday, when she had tripped over her own feet! No one would believe her mother had spent *mucho* money to give her ballet lessons for five years. In less than two days, she had proven to have the grace of an overfed anteater! Such things had never happened to her before, and even now,

they only happened when Travis was around.
It was better to stay far away from him; it was
just too humiliating otherwise.

Having made up her mind, she jumped out
of bed and headed toward the shower, eager to
get to the beach. Perhaps today, the undertow
would not be so strong.

The phone jangled and she reached across
the bed for it, falling in a heap on the soft
mattress. Who could be calling? "Hello?"

"What have you been doing that's made you
so breathless this morning?" Travis's voice
echoed low in her ear, sending ripples of
delight through her body. "Don't tell me you
exercise this early?"

"No." She chuckled. "I was on my way to
the shower and had to crawl over the bed to
get to the phone." Her voice was light; she
had suddenly forgotten everything she had
just resolved.

"I called to invite you to breakfast, but
perhaps you'd better stay where you are and
I'll come join you."

"Mr. Cameron! How dare you suggest such
a thing! I may be just a poor country girl, but
you, sir, are no traveling salesman!" she said
in her best imitation of a thick TV-Texas
drawl.

He laughed, and her heart leaped at the
warmth in his voice. "In that case, get down
here as quick as you can before I get any more
ideas. There's a breakfast buffet no one can
resist, unless they measure it against lovely
girls falling across beds!"

"Give me fifteen minutes," she assured him breathlessly.

"That's all you'll get, or I'll be up to get you!"

The shower felt brisk and tingling against her now warm skin. She hurried as fast as she could, slipping on a navy blue shirt and a white, full skirt with deep pockets. Her make-up was kept to a bare minimum, again thanks to yesterday's sun. She had the beginnings of a good tan and only a little mascara and a hint of pink lipstick were necessary to have her looking her best. She slipped her feet into small, low-heeled sandals just as a knock sounded in the quiet room. Thinking it was the housekeeping crew, she ran to the door with her hairbrush in her hand, arm in midair to stroke her unruly curls back into some semblance of order.

Travis stood against the doorjamb, eyes gleaming in appreciation of the picture she made, all crisp and wide-eyed and innocent.

"Blue and white become you," he murmured, stepping into the room. He glanced around, taking note of the rumpled bed and small, baby-doll pajamas still thrown on the covers. One eyebrow rose and a smile played around his lips as he looked at her, obviously imagining her in the tiny scraps of nylon.

"Give me a moment and I'll be ready. I didn't know I was behind schedule." She returned to the mirror, industriously brushing her hair back into the gypsy style which suited her face so well.

"You aren't late; I'm early." He turned and strolled to the balcony, taking note of the dinner tray still there. "You ate alone last night?"

"Me and Mr. Sunset," she confirmed, trying not to notice him walking up behind her.

Tension crackled in the small space between them, and Dannee expected to see shooting sparks as his hands rested gently on her shoulders. Instead of sparks filling the air, a warmth flooded her body. It was like sipping a rich brandy and savoring its taste. Their eyes met in the mirror's reflection, speaking volumes before the spell was broken by the sound of a child's laughter drifting up from the beach.

"I wish I had known you were alone," he murmured. "I would have invited you for a walk along the beach. It was too romantic to stroll alone."

"I thought Miranda said you had a business appointment last night?" Thank heaven her voice didn't crack!

"I did, but it didn't last *all* night."

His hand reached up, as if of its own accord, and stroked the back of her hair, his finger twining one of the curls into a small ringlet. His touch was doing strange things to her, making it hard to breathe, hard to move. His eyes caught hers in the mirror and he slowly smiled, looking like a satisfied cat.

She straightened her spine. Well, this was one book with a surprise ending! She wasn't going to fall all over him, figuratively, or literally—ever! He had enough women doing that already!

"Are you ready?" she questioned primly.

"Yes, but you may need more time," he murmured cryptically. He smiled again at her quizzical expression, which was quickly followed by a deep blush as she realized his meaning. "Come on! I promised to feed you and that's just what I plan to do."

They stepped off the elevator and Travis led her down the walkway, past the rope bridge and down a small set of stairs. She hadn't noticed the thatch-roofed restaurant before. It just seemed like part of the scenery. Besides, all along the walkways above were peacocks, proud to strut and show their feathers for the eyes of the watching tourists.

Large tables were set end to end across one side of the pavilion, covered with silver trays piled high, and straw baskets brimming with fruits and rolls, eggs, bacon and many varieties of fresh fruits, next to silver punch bowls and glasses filled with fresh juices. Travis held out a plate, his own gaze appreciative of her wide-eyed amazement at the vast selection.

"I suggest you try the Eggs Benedict." He nodded his head toward a silver warmer where perfectly round eggs, yolks bright yellow in the sun, sat on warm muffins, decorated with a slice of black olive. "They're quite the specialty, and very good."

"You mean those things that look like one-eyed monsters?"

"Yes," he said, and to emphasize the point, took the server and placed one on her plate. She tried not to look at it, but continued up the table, choosing sweet rolls, watermelon and cantaloupe slices, as well as papaya juice and bacon. They found a quiet table and Dannee looked down at her plate in wonder.

"If I eat all this, I'll get sick!"

"Thank goodness you didn't say fat! I'm tired of women who are always on diets."

"Are you intimating that women should be fat?"

"No. I'm saying that women should be women, not bean poles. Everyone needs something to cuddle. Thank heaven for teddy bears since most women are on constant diets."

"I can just see you with a teddy bear! Who are you kidding?"

Travis grinned. "Eat!" he ordered imperiously. "Starting with the Eggs Benedict. If you put it off until last, you might try the excuse that you're too full."

Meekly, she obeyed, closing her eyes as she placed it on her tongue, only to be pleasantly surprised at the delicious taste. "Mmmm . . ." she murmured, taking another bite, not looking at Travis's "I-told-you-so" expression.

She finished most of her fruits and sat, replete, sipping the delicious coffee with just a hint of cream. Then, for the first time, Dannee realized that Miranda wasn't there.

"Where's Miranda?" she asked casually, eyes darting around the restaurant to make certain she wasn't at another table. "I wouldn't expect her to miss a treat like this."

"Miranda has had a bout of *Turista*. Upset stomach and all that. She felt she should rest today, relax so she'll be able to join the cocktail party tonight," Travis explained, carefully watching her reaction.

Dannee's eyes darted nervously around the room, as if they were alone and she was afraid. Her smile was stiff, and Travis grimaced, as if he could read her mind. "Miranda is not my guardian, nor is she yours. Just relax and enjoy. I'm not trying to push you into deep water," he said calmly, picking up his roll and buttering it slowly.

"I don't like deep water. You never know the undertow is there until it's too late." She spoke without thinking, then blushed.

"My current will never take you further than you want to swim."

"Promise?"

"Promise. Now put your smile back on, we're going sightseeing."

She raised her brows, trying for a sophistication she really didn't have, only to receive a knowing look from Travis. "Really?"

"Yes, really."

He stood, his broad shoulders blocking out the sun reflecting from the pond behind him. He was so handsome, so devilish. And wasn't this supposed to be her holiday too? Why not go with him? She'd be able to keep the situation under control, surely. Some devil in her spoke a resounding "No," but she ignored it as she, too, stood. "Just give me two minutes to grab my bag."

"I'll give you five, as long as you don't change your mind." He smiled slowly, and once again, a warmth invaded her body, a warmth she couldn't ignore.

She turned quickly and strode through the crowd to the small garden path that led to her room, hoping he wouldn't notice how nervous her steps were as she tried to regain her composure. At least, she hadn't spilled anything on him!

Basically, Acapulco was a one main street tourist haven, but the difference between it and an American town could be felt as well as seen. The entire atmosphere was that of a sleepy, Spanish village almost oblivious of the many tourists who flocked to its shores.

They walked the length of the street, ignoring the line of hotels on one side, as they shopped on the other. Boats dipped and swayed in the small, circled and protected bay, making Dannee realize how many tourists must have been allowed into this vacation city on their yachts.

"Quite a tourist town, now." Travis spoke suddenly.

"Hasn't it always been?"

"Not in days gone by. In those days it was a

fort, surrounded by Indians, but not the kind
you're probably used to," he retorted dryly.
"Acapulco means 'Place where the reeds were
destroyed.'"

"And what does *that* mean?"

"No one knows for sure; but the supposition
is that there was an earthquake, or a tidal
wave that drove out the mainlanders and tore
down the reeds that used to crowd the
shores."

Dannee's gaze shifted to the small water-
way opening between the two cliffs that rose
to protect the almost circular harbor. "It's
hard to believe anything like that could have
happened here," she murmured.

"Perhaps," Travis stated. "At any rate, this
used to be the doorway to Asia, with ships
bringing in goods that would satisfy the rich-
est palate. Silks, velvets, gold jewelry, teas
and porcelains. Ships used to spend the winter months docked here, January through
February or March, before returning home."

"But how did the goods reach other areas?"

"By other ships and by pack, overland to the
Gulf of Mexico."

Dannee glanced behind her; the Sierra
Madres marched almost to the mouth of the
harbor. She could guess at the poverty of the
people as she noticed multi-colored stucco
buildings that had been broken into many
apartments. Chipped plaster and ragged
weeds belied the colorful facades.

"Poverty is everywhere. But as long as steps

are being taken to make it better, and they are, there's no time for sorrow." Travis spoke as if reading her mind.

They continued down the street as Dannee absorbed all the different sights and sounds that made Acapulco so foreign to her. Shops hung their wares outside on the awnings, and T-shirts, blouses and brightly embroidered children's outfits were displayed in the soft breeze. They ducked into one of the shops and Travis watched, grinning, while Dannee selected several T-shirts with an Acapulco sunset emblazoned across the front.

"These are for some of the girls at home. They love to wear shirts from different places, even though they haven't been there," she explained.

Travis lifted his cane and tapped one of the peasant blouses, covered with an abundance of embroidery in blues and greens. It was a simple blouse, but the handiwork made it special, and a souvenir worth having. Travis nodded to the proprietress, who took the blouse off the display and folded it carefully before wrapping it in brown paper. "Isn't that cheating?"

"Of course it's not!" Dannee retorted quickly, before realizing that the innocence in his eyes covered his mirth. She grinned, and Travis grinned back, making her feel special. Their eyes locked and for the moment there was only two of them in the whole world. She dropped her eyes, trying to hide the confusion written there. He had no right to affect her this way. And she had no right to allow him access to her emotions!

She glanced up again; his eyes were still on her. She forgot all her reasons for being careful and smiled. He turned away abruptly, and in doing so, startled her. She took a step backward, tripping over a low stool, and fell ignominiously to the floor, legs splayed in front of her like a rag doll.

Travis turned back and without thinking grabbed her up into his arms, holding her tight. "Are you all right?" he murmured, his hand stroking back the curls from her cheeks.

His genuine concern made her feel, once more, like a fool. She felt the hard leanness of his body, the slightly quickened pace of his heartbeat against the palm of her hand on his chest. "I'm fine. You startled me, that's all."

"Startled you? How did I do that?"

"By turning so fast. I thought your cane was going to hit me."

Travis tilted her chin with his fingers, laughing into her face. "Oh? And do your parents beat you? Or is there some other reason for your nerves to be so on edge?"

The proprietress, a small peasant woman, smiled benignly, crossing her hands over her ample stomach. She watched with interest through eagle eyes, obviously uncertain of what was being said, but she knew instinctively that it had to do with romance. She could tell by the gleam in the eyes of the tall stranger, and the blushing cheeks of the pretty young girl. What could be better than a romance blooming under her very own nose?

"Nonsense!" Dannee stated, keeping her expression bland. She wasn't going to let him know for anything in the world just how much his proximity disturbed her. "If you'll let me go, I'll get my bags and then we can have a cool drink in that sidewalk café next door. I imagine your foot must be needing a rest by now."

His arms dropped to his side immediately, and she could feel the withdrawl of his warmth, even in this tropical temperature. "By all means, let's have a drink." He paid for the blouse and tucked it nonchalantly under one arm before following her to the outdoor café.

They ordered Mexican beer and drank it straight from the bottle. Travis kept the conversation going at first by telling her some interesting facts about Acapulco and discussing other places he had been, things he had seen. Within fifteen minutes, Dannee had forgotten their earlier awkwardness and began to enjoy herself once again. A young boy, dark-skinned, black-eyed, wandered by their table, arms clasping a large sailing ship carved out of coconut bark and rigged with string. The workmanship was beautiful, and Dannee's eyes lit with excitement as she imagined her brother's pleasure in such a gift.

She clasped Travis's arm and didn't even

notice his surprise at the gesture. "Please! Ask him where he got that boat, Travis. Please, quickly, before he passes!"

Within seconds, the amazed little boy was across the street, streaking down the sandy beach, toes digging into the sand as he waved a sheaf of pesos above his head, calling out the good news to his friends.

"We'd better get out of here before his friends begin to pester us with other wonderful things to buy."

"You didn't have to buy it from him, you know. I just wanted to know where to buy one." Her glance shifted to the boat, now resting in the center of the table. "But I'm glad you did. It's a fine piece of workmanship," she added softly, reaching for her purse. "Now, how much did you pay him?" she asked in a businesslike tone, scrambling through the bills in her purse.

"It's my gift to your brother. And this," he handed her the wrapped shirt, "is for you." He stilled the protest on her lips by raising his glass and sipping a salute. "Now, let's go!"

A waiting taxi drove them back to the Princess, following the mountain road that allowed Dannee a perfect view of the Acapulco skyline and bay.

She leaned back, sighing happily.

"The day is not yet over, Miss Hathaway. When we get back, I want you to change into your bathing suit and meet me in the waterfall bar in fifteen minutes. The day has, in fact, just begun. . . ."

Chapter Six

A young blond man walked through the curtain of water and took one of the underwater bar stools directly across from Dannee, obviously hoping to gain her attention. She continued to twirl her glass on the slick bar surface and stare unseeingly toward the corner of the waterfall, only absently aware of the young man's scrutiny as he attempted to catch her eye. She glanced up and gave him a smile, and he responded with such eagerness that Dannee half-expected him to jump the bar between them. He grinned ruefully and his eyes held the promise of meeting her again, making her chuckle. She knew he was pleased with what he saw but she was unaffected by it. Why didn't his admiration have the same effect as Travis's? Her chuckle died at that thought. Stop it! she admonished herself. Travis was just trying to be a friend, nothing more. He was way out of her league and she knew it. And no doubt so did he. All he wanted was a companion, someone to help him pass the time while the beautiful Miranda was ill.

The hair rose on her nape, making her turn toward the direction of the door. Travis stood at the entrance of the bar, hands low on his hips as he listened to a full-blown older woman who had an apparent problem with her eyelashes. They kept batting in the breeze as she gazed at him with adoration. Her hands fluttered in quick staccato movements, making her look like a puppet on a string. A sharp pain made itself felt in the pit of Dannee's stomach as she watched him smile slowly, extricating himself from her grasp. He quirked an eyebrow at Dannee and strolled slowly toward her. His eyes told her he knew she had watched the whole scene and knew what she felt about it.

"Some women need more 'help' than others," he stated blandly in answer to her unspoken question, a grin tugging at the corner of his mouth. Darn him for accurately reading her thoughts!

"Some men need to turn off their sex appeal around those less fortunate," she returned haughtily.

77

"Why, Dannee, are you intimating that I have sex appeal?" He frowned in mock severity. "Shame on you for noticing such a vulgar asset, but I'll be gentlemanly and reciprocate by saying so do you."

"Oh, be quiet!"

"Temper, temper." He grinned, waving aside the bartender. "Are you ready?"

"Where are we going?"

"You'll see."

He reached for her hands, which were clasped tightly in her lap. She tried to refuse his hold, not wanting him to touch her for fear of that warm feeling that invaded her bones. Better to have no contact at all than to give away her feelings. But it was not in the cards for her. He reached down and took her hands in his, drawing her up to stand next to him. She would have loved to wipe the smile from his face as he watched her reaction flit across her features.

She turned and retraced her steps to the door, ignoring the thudding of her heart. "Are you always so bossy?"

"Yes. And if you didn't like it, you wouldn't have been here, waiting for me," he stated calmly, shutting off any comment she could have made before she had a chance to make it. They followed the narrow, twisting walkway past the large pool and down the rock steps to the beach. He led and she followed, her hand comfortably ensconced in his.

She smiled to herself. No one at home

would believe it if they saw her complacently following in his footsteps, like an Indian squaw with her warrior. She had never been one to follow before and was surprised that she liked it, even felt satisfied with it.

"And what is going through that pretty head of yours to make you smile? Thinking up a new way to spill something on me?"

Anger flared. "No, I'm trying to figure out how I can drown you!"

"You won't have to wonder much longer." He pointed to a gaily striped sailboat that two boys were pushing to the water's edge. "That's ours for the rest of the afternoon, along with the food in that hamper." He pointed back toward the hotel, shining like a temple in the early afternoon sun. Walking along the same path they had just traveled was a young Mexican girl in uniform, a large wicker basket on her arm. One of the boys ran to meet her and she passed the basket on to him. Dannee could see the slim neck of a bottle peeking out of the side of the hamper and smiled. It looked like part of a seduction scene in an old movie—boy—girl—sailboat in a small cove—wine—bread. The only thing missing was music and certainly the movie crew could provide that! She laughed.

Suddenly her attention returned to the sailboat that was even now being pushed into the water, and it sank into her head that Travis had meant what he had just said. They were really going sailing!

"Really?" she squeaked excitedly, looking suddenly like a small child just given a large treat.

He smiled indulgently. "Yes, really."

Her expression fell and she looked up at him, forgetting her earlier anger as she became lost in the blueness of his eyes.

"What is it?" he asked softly and she broke their gaze to stare at a button on his shirt, a small nervous smile on her face.

"I'm sure you planned all this with Miranda in mind, and I'm sure it's wonderful fun, but I don't know how to sail. I've never done it before."

"The boat is only ten feet long and has one small sail, small enough to be handled by one person," he said confidently, his arrogance once again in the forefront. "If you want to learn, then I can teach you all you need to know."

"O.K.," she said, smiling once again, "but don't blame me if I capsize us!"

"Ready?" His hand cupped her elbow and he led her toward the water's edge, helping her keep her balance as she stepped over the side and into the boat. He handed her the hamper and gave a mighty shove to the back of the boat, pushing it into the water until it floated free of the sand beneath, then jumped in over the side. He immediately began adjusting the sail, allowing the wind to fill the red- and yellow-striped canvas, which billowed gaily in the breeze.

"There's a radio in the hamper if you can't stand the quiet."

Of course! Since a movie crew wasn't here, he would have to have a radio to fill in! "I like the quiet. Unless you can't live without the noisy beat in your ears?"

"No, the noisy beat isn't to my taste." He grinned. "I prefer other, more sophisticated noises."

She ignored him. Darn the man! She always seemed to walk into a set-up straight from vaudeville, with herself as the straight man.

The small boat skimmed across the water, dipping slightly as it crested each small wave. Travis adjusted the sail, his lean, muscular legs taut as he balanced. He wore white shorts and a red and white knit shirt that molded his body, showing his powerful build to advantage. She wondered if he knew what a devastating effect he had on women, then decided that it was something so natural to him that he probably didn't even give it a second thought.

"Where's your cane?"

"At the hotel. I only need it when I walk a lot. The foot's almost better, anyway."

"You look like an ad for a yacht club." She pushed her windblown hair away from her face, tilting her chin toward the sun as she watched him easily maneuver the sail.

"Would you settle for anything less?"

"Of course not!" she teased. "I only date yachtsmen or up-and-coming executives. I know that's rather hard to do in El Paso since the selection, as well as large bodies of water, is limited, but I don't waver in my standards." Her teasing voice was clear, her eyes bright with mischief.

"Right. That's why I'm your first date!" he teased back with a gleam in his eyes. "I haven't been anyone's first date in years."

"Well, you won't be my last, believe me. You've opened a whole new vista for me. New horizons and all that sort of thing." She watched his mouth clench as he adjusted the sail and knew she had scored a hit. How dare he be so conceited as to say she had no boyfriends, even in jest! Who did he think he was, Prince Charming? Well, she wasn't Cinderella! Yes, she was, a little voice niggled in the back of her mind, but she ignored it.

Two large, black island-like boulders were fast rising directly in front of them, distracting her attention from her anger of just minutes ago. She was amazed at the size of them. From the shore they had looked so small, like tiny little islands in a pretend sea. The water lapped gently at their bases, turning the stone from a dark gray to glistening black. The boat skimmed between them as Travis adjusted the sail so the wind would turn the boat to follow the edge of the cove, readjusting the placement of the sail once again, so the craft tilted slightly to the left.

"Port," he stated quietly, merriment dancing in his eyes as he watched her surprised expression.

"How did you know I was wondering?"

"I'm a mind reader when it comes to you."

The heck he was! Her eyes flashed angrily at his arrogant assumption, but he grinned and the momentary anger she felt was swept away by his warmth, only to return again at his next words.

"No, I won't go there, and yes, I am arrogant."

"I didn't know I was so transparent. It must be boring for you."

"Oh, no, not boring. Never boring," he murmured, and it felt like a caress. The wind ruffled her hair, drifting it back from her cheeks to show her fine bone structure as she stared up at the sail, afraid to look at him for fear of what he might see in her eyes. They sailed around the headland and into another cove and Travis made ready to land, bringing them into the far side of a deserted beach.

It looked as if it had never been touched by humans, and as they waded the last few feet to shore, pulling the boat onto the beach, she couldn't help a small exclamation at the beauty surrounding them. "Oh, how lovely," she breathed, turning toward Travis. He stood slightly behind her, his hand on the bow of the boat, and watched her with narrowed, intense eyes.

"Isn't it, though?" His eyes never left her, traveling slowly down her slim body, only to return to her flushed face.

"But then, I imagine you bring all your girls here?" she asked in a sugar-sweet voice, just to let him know she was not allowing him to put his mark on her.

"All of them," he repeated solemnly as he walked up to her side, towering above her and cutting off her air with his very presence. "And some that aren't—yet."

Dannee stifled the urge to step on his foot—hard—and bent to pick up the hamper of food. But he was there before her and as their hands touched a shock like an electric current shot through her body, making her jump away. His eyebrow rose in question, but she kept her face averted. Travis gave a shrug and began walking up the beach to a small clearing next to a large, smooth rock.

Travis unfolded the blanket he had tucked under his arm and with a snap of his wrist spread it out on the sand. He was certainly adept at that, Dannee thought, as she placed the hamper next to the blanket. With silent consent, they both stripped off their outer clothing to the bathing suits they wore underneath, neither looking at the other, or so it seemed to Dannee.

They swam in the clear blue water, so still compared to the larger cove they had just left. No matter what its depth, the water was crystal clear, making the bottom seem only a few feet away instead of a few fathoms. The sand sparkled like a thousand small diamonds that had been ground up and scattered by wind and surf. It was just as she had always envisioned an Acapulco vacation to be, right down to the gorgeous man floating beside her, Dannee thought. They both headed for shore at the same time, walking up the slope toward the small area they had chosen.

She could feel the heat of the sun drying her body almost immediately and she glanced up to see the tiny scraps of clouds, noticing instead just how close Travis stood next to her. The hair on the back of her neck rose, warning her of intense danger. They had walked halfway to the blanket before his arm snaked out and stopped her, swinging her around to face him. He wore a puzzled expression, his brow furrowed with unspoken questions.

"Are you afraid of me?"

"Of course not!" she exclaimed, fervently wishing he would let her go.

"Then why do you shy away every time I touch you or get near you? Do I repel you?"

"I just don't like to be touched, that's all."

"I don't believe it."

"I don't have to prove it."

"Don't you, Dannee?" There was a thread of steel in his voice to match the steely glint in his hard blue eyes. "Don't you?" He tightened his grip on her and lowered his mouth to meet hers in a brief, bruising kiss. Fire shot through her limbs and she moaned softly; no man had ever made her feel this way before.

And no man would make her feel this way now! she promised herself. Certainly not this man, who had another woman waiting for him. He was only teasing her, anyway; she

should have known better than to have dared
him as she had. She would say nothing; she
would pretend this had never even happened.
She tore herself out of his grasp and ran up
the beach, plopping down on the blanket and
burrowing into the hamper, ignoring her
shaking hands. Travis took a seat beside her
as he watched her with narrowed eyes.

The food was delicious. The hotel had
packed *tacos el carbon,* flour tortillas stuffed
with charcoal cooked pork and beef, toma-
toes, fresh slices of melon along with other
fruits and a deep, rich, red wine. It was a
meal fit for a king and even Travis's overwhelming presence couldn't stop her from
enjoying the food.

Gradually, the stiltedness between them
dissolved as they ate. After all, Dannee
thought with a small smile, how could she
stay mad when she had good food, good wine
and was with a man who knew his place? She
glanced over at Travis. He was propped
against the large rock, his eyes drooping as he
contemplated the swirling red wine in his
glass. He was at least three feet away from
her. So what if he was just looking for a
stand-in while Miranda was ill? She was here
and the bogeyman hadn't gotten her yet, had
he? She might as well make the most of her
vacation and carry home memories that
would warm her on the long, cold El Paso
nights. Travis moved and Dannee glanced up
at him through her lashes. He stretched out
on the blanket, his hands behind his head and

his eyes closed. He looked like a little boy when he rested, the lines of tension eased and the steely blue eyes with the x-ray vision closed. His lashes really were too long. They should have belonged to a girl. Darn him! Did he have to have everything? She silently wished him a hangnail and took a sip of her wine, closing her eyes as she placed the glass next to her. Just at that moment, Travis took his arm from behind his head and pushed himself up, catching the glass in midair. In slow motion, they watched it slip out of her hands as large drops of wine ran down his arm and across her breasts, making her jump a little at the coolness.

"Blast!" he muttered, scrambling for the glass before it spilled the rest of its contents on them. He balanced it, looked up and smiled. "Three times a charm, I wonder?"

Her eyes filled with tears of embarrassment. "If you hadn't moved—" She swallowed hard, trying to remove the lump in her throat.

His hand rose and gently touched the side of her face. "Don't cry, Dannee. It was only a silly accident. There's more wine."

She glanced up to explain, but the words died on her lips as she became lost in his warm, blue eyes. How could she ever have thought they were hard steel?

A tear trickled down the side of her cheeks, but she didn't move, nor did he. They were suspended in time and space together. Everything else was forgotten in the midst of the moment. His mouth was inches from hers, his warm breath fanning her slightly parted lips. His head came closer and suddenly his lips were on hers, tenderly but firmly, seeking a response she knew she would give. His tongue moved like live fire against hers, filling her whole body with the heat of molten lava. He gathered her closer, pressing her breasts against his chest. Her arms encircled his waist, reveling in the touch of skin against skin. She was drowning in sensations and feelings she had never experienced before. Nothing else mattered except that he continue to hold her, touch her, kiss her, allowing her to die in such a lovely way. She could feel his fast beating heart and knew her own was beating in unison. One hand cupped her head, fingers tangling in the dark curls as he pressed her closer. She had never experienced such intense passion before, and nothing mattered except to keep this moment alive.

His hand wandered over her back, stopping to unclasp the catch of her bathing suit before pushing the offending fabric out of the way. She moaned slightly as his hand curved to tease and stroke her warm breast. Warning bells rang in the back of her mind, but she couldn't seem to hear them clearly. With each touch of his lean fingertips, with every dart of his tongue, the passion rose. His hand became deliberate, more searching, and she paid no heed to what he was doing, only to the sensations he aroused. His lips left hers and made a heated trail down her cheek to her neck. Her fingers tangled in his jet black hair, wanting him to go on and on and never stop.

"You taste like wine," he murmured softly as he put a finger beneath the restricting band of her bikini bottoms. His voice suddenly broke the spell, bringing her back to earth with a thud.

"No!" She grabbed his hand, stopping the downward movement. She was torn between the feelings that were still charging through her system and the knowledge that she would hate herself tomorrow.

His head rose from its sanctuary and eyes that were still warm with feeling showed his puzzlement. "No? You want me as much as I want you. Don't bother to deny it."

"I won't," she confessed. "But that doesn't mean that I can go through with it." She didn't move from her place, but she kept her eyes averted from his. She was too embarrassed to look at him.

"Why?"

She sat up as he released her from the pressure of his body and fumbled for the catch on her bikini top with trembling hands. Her eyes were misty. He was right; she *had* acted as if she would go along with whatever he wanted—and she might have, if his words hadn't broken the spell. Guilt flamed in her face.

"I see. A regular tease. You play this game often?" His voice was filled with contempt, rasping out the words like small poisoned darts that struck at her to make tiny pinpricks in her conscience.

"I've never played the game before." The words caught in her throat.

There was a moment of stunned silence, then his fingers gently lifted her chin and his blue eyes, bright with questions, looked into her glistening brown ones. His anger and bitterness dissolved. "Why didn't you stop me sooner?" he asked softly.

"There wasn't much time for that."

"I'm sorry, Dannee. I never would have started this if I had known."

"It was just as much my fault as it was yours. I should have stopped you," she muttered, as she clasped her still shaking knees. He must think her childish compared to his own sophistication!

"I should have known better." He gave a crooked smile that made Dannee's heart do a flip-flop. "I just got carried away. You're a beautiful woman, in case you don't know it."

"Not as beautiful as Miranda." She bit her lip; what a stupid thing to say!

"No, not as beautiful as Miranda. But since when can one compare apples and oranges?" he teased, and she smiled. Travis stood and reached out a hand to her. "Come on, let's rinse off this wine. I've played the unicorn long enough."

"Unicorn?" She stared up at him, clearly unable to understand his analogy. He turned, and they slowly walked down the beach toward the sea.

"In medieval times, the unicorn was described as a fierce fighter that would even attack elephants and in one blow could disable any opponent. The only way hunters could catch him was to leave a young virgin in the forest. When the unicorn saw her, he would run toward her and lie down at her feet, with his head in her lap, in fact, and so was captured by the hunters."

They had reached the water. The warm water lapped at Dannee's ankles as they slowly waded in deeper. She kept her head bent and watched the slowly swirling water play on the silver sand beneath.

"Dannee, look at me." She raised her eyes, momentarily blinded by the sun behind him. His lips briefly touched hers, but before she could react, he was pulling her into the center of the small cove. "Let's swim!"

She gave a sigh of relief. The atmosphere was once again bearable. She forced herself to put the earlier scene out of her mind. She giggled as she thought of the unicorn. "And the moral of the story is never go near a young and beautiful virgin!"

"No. The moral of the story is never to haunt woods where there are hunters!" He flashed a grin at her before diving underwater, only to appear a moment later with glistening hair and tanned, glowing skin.

They played, then rested before setting off

once more for the hotel. It had been so relaxing, barring that one, disturbing scene. And now their relationship was on another level altogether, and Dannee had no idea where she stood at all.

They rounded the coastline and she could immediately see the hotel glistening in the late afternoon sun. On a long stretch of beach just to the right of the private grounds was a large red and white striped parachute floating in the air parallel to the shoreline.

Chapter Seven

"Look!" she shouted excitedly.

Travis's eyes lit with amusement as he watched her gaze dart from the parachutist high in the sky to the gaily painted jeep that pulled him along the shore of the harbor.

"Would you like to try it?" His tone was indulgent, but she didn't notice as she watched the descent of the harnessed man. The parachute glided down slowly, allowing the man, who Dannee now saw was older than she had at first imagined, to flex his knees to take the small jolt as he returned to earth.

"Try it? I'd love to! After all, *he* doesn't seem the worse for wear!" she exclaimed.

"Give me a few minutes." Travis turned

and made arrangements for the small sail-boat to be docked and cleaned, and the now empty hamper of food to be taken back to the kitchen with his compliments and a hefty tip. But Dannee was oblivious to all of it as she watched a young boy fold the parachute while an older one unfastened the straps from the parachutist.

Soon they were on their way across the hot sand, running hand in hand toward the jeep. Travis spoke quickly to the older Mexican boy, rattling along in Spanish as if he had spoken it all his life. She couldn't follow the conversation but watched Travis's face, marveling at his looks, the smile curving his lips, the dimples as he grinned in understanding of the jeep driver's instructions. Travis suddenly turned to her, holding out his hand to help her into the back seat.

"Come on, we have to go further down the beach before you can fly, *mi chiquita*." *My little one*. She warmed at the tone of his voice.

The jeep's engine was gunned and the driver gave the wheel a sharp turn, spinning the tires in the soft, fluffy sand as they bumped further down the beach in the same direction as she had taken her horseback ride the day before. The wind was hot as it ruffled her hair and her cheeks were pink, but not from the heat as much as from the excitement. Travis sat close to her, his hand still holding hers. The Acapulco sun was just beginning to lower itself into the sea, but first, as if to remind everyone of nature's glories, the hot rays shaded into a spectacular pattern of colors.

The jeep slowed, then stopped and reversed. The young boy, probably in his early teens, jumped out and reached for the red and white striped silk while the driver began unwinding the rope. Travis helped Dannee out and they walked to the spot the boy pointed out. She had no time to reconsider her hasty decision. She swallowed hard and allowed herself to be strapped around the legs and over the chest, the harness fitting snugly against her slim form. Travis translated the boy's instructions and she was told to hold on to two looped straps while the boy straightened out the parachute, readying it to receive the light breeze. The driver snaked the rope between her and the jeep, making sure it was securely tied to the back of the car. Travis stood by, and she gave him a brave smile as the driver called to him. Apparently he was riding in comfort, with both feet on the floorboards, while she had nothing between herself and the ground!

Within moments, the jeep was slowly pulling away, leaving her to stand on the lonely beach and wonder if the thin material that billowed behind her would really pull her up and keep her there, or if she would be dragged along the beach as they continued to drive toward the hotel. She watched the long coil of rope uncurl and suddenly panic enveloped her.

"Wait!" she cried, but it was too late, the line was unwound and stretched taut, and she had no choice but to do as she had been instructed. She took one step forward and before she could place the other foot down, she was in the air, lifted higher and higher in a gentle arc as the wind filled the chute and carried her over the heads of a group of young Mexican boys playing in the sand. She hung between heaven and earth. The sky was bluer, the small tufts of clouds whiter, the sand more shimmery from that height than ever before. The water was as clear as ever. She could see the shelf of sand go out forever until it dropped out of sight in the faraway deep water. She turned her head toward the grassy dunes, now able to see where the road wound itself from the airport to the small, sleepy town.

The view from her lofty height was so panoramic and breathtaking that Dannee suddenly knew why people took up skydiving as a hobby. The feeling of floating was heavenly. She looked down at her hands, surprised to find them clutching the straps so tightly. She was supposed to pull them if she wanted to go from one side to the other, so why was she holding them as if the parachute would drop if she let go?

She could see Travis seated in the jeep, though she could barely make out his face, as they raced along the beach. "Don't disgrace yourself now, Dannee girl," she whispered to the wind.

The hotel was now on her right, still towering above her. How close it seemed! Yet she wasn't worried. It was as if floating in the air was the answer to all her problems. She was even with the tops of the palm trees that sheltered the thatched cabanas along the front of the hotel when the jeep began slowing down. Immediately, she began descending.

A small boy, naked except for a pair of blue shorts, ran in her shadow, shouting Spanish words of encouragement. At least, she hoped that was what they were! She dropped slowly to earth, the parachute beginning to fold behind her as the wind itself was not sufficient to keep it aloft. There was no jarring, no fast descent. In fact, there had been nothing to be afraid of at all! The boy quickly reached for her chute and began to fold it, nodding his head and keeping up a constant stream of Spanish. She looked up to find Travis at her side, smiling.

"He says you were a pro, and doesn't the *señorita* do this all the time?" he translated.

"First time," she said to the small boy. "But there's a first time for *everything!*"

"There certainly is," Travis murmured softly as he undid her harness, his hand brushing gently against her breast and sending a tingle throughout her body. She looked at his face as he unhooked her, wondering if she could have mistaken his meaning. But when he glanced up at her, she knew she had been right. Their eyes locked, making her aware of the fact that he was as conscious of her as she was of him.

"Unless you're out to catch unicorns!"

"Remember that it was a *young* virgin, not an old one."

A wide-faced peasant woman made her way to their side. She jabbed a black plastic case filled with every size and description of rings under Dannee's nose and jabbered away as if they were old friends. Her black eyes slyly glanced at Travis from time to time, but she continued her speech to Dannee. When she received no reaction, she chose one and pushed it toward Dannee, immediately switching to English.

"Beautiful ring, no? Cheap price, only fifty-five dollars, American." The old woman nodded her head to emphasize her price.

"No, too much," Dannee stated, handing it back as she tried to dismiss the woman, but persistence seemed to be the order of the day.

She shrugged her shoulders. "Fifty, then." She pushed the ring into Dannee's hand.

"Too much," Dannee said again, handing it back yet again as she continued to walk toward the steps leading to the hotel.

"Thirty. Bottom rock," the old lady called out to her and she turned, sorely tempted, before realizing she had no money with her. Travis seemed to know immediately, and spoke up.

"I'll buy it for the *señorita*." He pulled out his wallet and slipped the woman the correct bills over Dannee's protests.

"Nonsense," he stated, ending their argument. "It's a souvenir of our day together." He grinned before leaning down and placing his lips on hers, melting any resistance she might have felt. He lifted her hand and placed the ring on her finger. It was almost a ceremony, as if they were becoming engaged. . . .

She tried to lighten the mood, ignoring the turquoise and silver ring that, to her, glistened as brightly as any diamond.

"Just how rich are you that you can throw away so much money?"

"Just enough to make ends meet and have some left over for thirty-dollar rings."

"I'm serious!"

"Didn't your mother ever tell you it was rude to ask questions like that?"

"I just want to know if I should offer to pay for the ring I didn't offer to buy. I don't want to offend you, but I don't want to accept something that you worked hard for, either," she said primly, looking down at her hand where the ring now rested. It fit her to a tee; hammered silver with a large square of turquoise gleamed against the tan of her long fingers.

"Yes, I earned it, and no, I don't want you to offer to pay me," he said imperiously, deliberately misunderstanding her. "Now, get cleaned up and I'll meet you in the lobby in exactly an hour. Next on the agenda is the sunset cruise."

"Are you going, too?"

"Yes. One naive El Paso girl is too much for the Acapulco natives to cope with, especially

one as accident-prone as you." His hand went
to his chest as if remembering the slushy
drink and the wine that had been dumped on
him within the last two days. Dannee's
cheeks flushed with embarrassment. Beast!
He didn't have to remind her just how clumsy
she could be! She walked toward the main
desk, her back ramrod stiff, and in a flash
remembered how she had stepped on his foot
that first day. Somehow, it brought the whole
episode into perspective. She glanced over her
shoulder, laughing up at him.

"Gentlemen *never* recount their date's *faux
pas* to the world, sir!"

"Certainly not!" His eyes gleamed with
hidden mischief. "Are you saying that you're a
woman of the world and I'm a gentleman?"

"Since neither is true, I'd be a liar, wouldn't
I?" she retorted impishly. "An' my Momma
didn't raise no liar, suh!" she drawled at him,
then darted off to catch the elevator which
was just closing, leaving him standing in the
lobby with a grin on his face.

She continued to smile all the way to her
floor, almost giggling to herself as she un-
locked the door and collapsed on the bed. How
wonderful it had been to share the day with
him! She better watch out, though, it could
become a habit. And once Miranda was
well . . .

The other woman's name brought Dannee
quickly down to earth. Beautiful Miranda, for
whom she had been filling in all day. If
Miranda had been with him on the beach,

would she have spilled wine all over him?
Would he have gone further in his lovemaking, tormenting her with heat and flame?
Would they have pursued their feelings to the
ultimate consummation in the hot tropical
sand as if they were Adam and Eve in their
own deserted Eden?

The thought of Miranda in Travis's arms
hurt so much that Dannee crossed her arms
over her stomach. All the laughter of the
afternoon was gone as pictures flashed
through her mind like a movie shown in slow
motion. Oh, how it hurt to think of Travis and
Miranda—together.

She stood resolutely. Enough of these
thoughts. She had the cruise in front of her
tonight and she had all day tomorrow to
worry about the consequences of their relationship. Right now, she would take what
time she had left with Travis and make the
most of it. This was her dream vacation,
wasn't it?

Chapter Eight

The dock was filled with tourists waiting to board the triple-decker sightseeing yacht; but while everyone else waited patiently with ticket in hand, Travis had whisked her to the front of the line and talked to the man in charge. Within seconds, their conversation, conducted entirely in Spanish, was over and they were escorted up the ramp by the ticket man and shown to the best seats on the boat, on the top deck. The rest of the crowd still thronged behind them.

Drinks were handed to them, the rest of the tourists boarded, the engines revved up and the ship slowly chugged away from the dock, gently swaying, top-heavy, through the calm harbor waters toward the opening to the ocean.

The seats quickly filled all around them. Others were handed drinks as well and an air of festivity surrounded them. Dannee glanced at Travis through her lashes. Could he possibly be enjoying himself? His eyes were covered with sunglasses and his face gave no clue to his feelings as he stared across the water to the cliffs. Houses dangling like unstrung pearls and scattered on the steep incline found small pockets in the rock in which to rest their rambling foundations.

"And over to your right, ladies and gentlemen," the tour guide's voice droned just above the din of the motor, "is the area that was chiseled out of the rock so the soft, Pacific breeze could find its way to our shores and provide us with nature's air conditioning. The pearl divers now give a fantastic and thrilling show there every weekend. . . ."

Dannee sipped her drink, suddenly aware of Travis's eyes resting on her, his glasses in his hand. She could feel the pull of the afternoon's magic working once again, tugging at her as strongly as the invisible, but strong undertow. At his unspoken command, she raised her eyes to meet his, and they both smiled slowly, lost in their own world among the hundreds of tourists. A delicious shiver ran down her spine.

"Cold?" he asked, slipping his arm around her shoulder and holding her close.

"Mmmm." Why explain that his nearness did funny, wonderful things to her?

"What does that mean in plain English?"

"That I'm not cold, but this is more comfortable," she teased, surprised that she felt no embarrassment at her honesty. It earned her another smile that dimpled his cheek and made her feel even more honey-sweet and warm than before.

An older couple seated across from them caught Dannee's eyes and she grinned in greeting to her fellow tourists. The older woman's elbow found her spouse's rib and dug in. "Look," she whispered in a voice that could have rivaled the tour guide with his megaphone. "Newlyweds!"

"Ugh," he grunted. "What are they doing on this thing then? I remember where we spent our honeymoon, and it wasn't taking in the sights!" he retorted loud enough so that it seemed like everyone's attention was focused on Dannee and Travis.

She turned dark crimson and wanted to hide somewhere. Anywhere! Travis's chest moved, rumbling in laughter, before a small fist plummeted into his mid-section to send out a "whouff" of air. He grabbed her hand, holding it surprisingly gently in his, his thumb circling her palm. His lips brushed gently against her temple, his breath was warm on her skin. She knew he could feel her accelerated pulse and wondered if his was as erratic. Suddenly, she stiffened. He was putting on a show for these people! He was deliberately pretending that they *were* newly-weds, just for the fun of it! Dannee pulled out of his embrace, the wind cooling her fevered skin.

His voice seemed to come from far away. "What's the matter, darling?"

"I'm fine," she choked. "I am *not* your 'darling' and I don't enjoy being made to look a fool in your little game."

He didn't pretend not to understand her. "Does it bother you so much?"

"Pretending something when it's not the case always bothers me."

"My, my. I take it you never played with paper dolls."

"That's not the same thing!"

"Then, would you rather they think we came here on an assignation that had nothing to do with marriage? People like stories, Dannee. They're not going to believe what you want them to, only what seems obvious to them." He shrugged his shoulders. "I just thought one evil was better than the other," he stated coolly.

"You're awful!" she hissed, smiling sweetly beneath eyes that sparkled dangerously.

"I'm awful good," he murmured. "Otherwise your pulse wouldn't be racing the way it is."

She was speechless for a moment, unable to think of anything but her frustrated anger. Without thinking, she tipped her glass, releasing the last of the liquid over his trousers.

"If you're so good, what in the name of

heaven are you doing here with me, when you could obviously be with someone whose talents match your own?"

She heard his gasp and ignored it. "Why you . . ."

She stood quickly and walked to the bow of the ship, her muscles rigid with anger.

She refused the tears that wanted to fall, holding them in to form a lump in her throat. She couldn't understand why such a silly thing could make her feel so angry and hurt, but it did. She hoped he fell overboard, hoped he'd drown, hoped—hoped he'd come after her and apologize.

No! No! No! Her hands clasped the railing tightly, knuckles turning white with the exertion. She knew what the problem was. She, Dannee Hathaway, the one who swore she would never fall in love and become a victim of the tyrannical guidance of another, had done just that!

"Are you through being angry?" His voice was low, almost with a hint of laughter, but it couldn't be. He must be angry with her for spilling her drink on him intentionally. It wasn't bad enough that she had done it accidentally so many times before, this time, she had deliberately doused him.

"I'm sorry about the drink."

"I'm not. It seems the only time you give me a real dousing is when it's accidental. When it's intentional, the glass is empty. Except for a few ice cubes, it was harmless enough."

She stared straight ahead, distantly hearing

the guide describe the fabulous home the boat was slowly chugging past, her attention completely turned to the man at her side.

"I'm sorry about teasing you earlier. I didn't mean any harm."

"I'm sorry I got mad. I didn't really mean to spill my drink again."

His chuckle rumbled deep in his throat. "Yes, you did. But now that we've both said our 'sorries,' let's forget it."

"Yes, you're right, I did." She turned and looked up at him. "It's just that—that—" She searched for words, but before she could find them, his finger was on her lips, silencing her.

"It doesn't matter. Let's just enjoy the rest of the cruise."

She nodded her head, not trusting her voice.

"It's been such a perfect day, let's not spoil it now."

Spoil it? It had already been spoiled the moment she realized she was in love with him. And she was hurt all the more by the fact that he had acted as if he loved her in return. He was just having a fun time with a substitute, right now, but when Miranda was feeling better . . .

"Miranda should be here."

He nodded his head. "She'd enjoy this."

"She's very special to you, isn't she?" What was she trying to do? Beat herself to death emotionally?

"Very."

They spent the rest of the tour quietly standing at the bow. The sunset was beautiful as the flaming globe rested briefly on the watery horizon before quickly passing out of view. Dannee tried to be properly impressed, but a portion of her mind had withdrawn, hiding far away from the hurt she knew was waiting for her not far ahead.

Two more days to go and her vacation would be over. And if that wasn't enough, Miranda would be at the party tonight—on Travis's arm—enjoying the comfort of his presence while Dannee watched them—alone.

Chapter Nine

The large mirror above the dresser told Dannee she looked her best. The long sea-blue dress clung softly to her curves, accenting the slim shapeliness of her figure. The small cap sleeves and deep square neckline molded her breasts and the empire cut made her seem taller than she was. She turned gracefully, watching the soft fabric swish around her calves. If this dress didn't catch Travis's attention, then nothing would. Dannee wanted to see his glow of appreciation. She wanted him to want to hold her as much as she ached to be held. She wanted him. . . .

Dannee raised her hand in the air, staring at the lovely turquoise and silver ring. It was perfect for her, just the right size and color.

She remembered the look on his face when she had finally accepted it. Did it mean the same thing to him as it meant to her? Certainly not an engagement ring, but perhaps a promise of their future friendship? Surely he wouldn't have bothered to buy it for her unless he cared; would he? He *had* to feel that undeniable attraction between them, just as much as she did.

She dropped her hand, slipping a small silver purse under her arm. As she walked to the door and flicked off the lights, her thoughts were still on Travis. She was just going to a party and that was that, she told herself. One kiss does not a lover make. Besides, what was wrong with her? She had never wanted any man to do what she had visions of Travis doing to her. Her feelings fluctuated back and forth all the way down to the lobby. Dannee almost chuckled aloud as she envisioned a little angel on one shoulder and a little devil on the other, just like in the cartoons. She wanted Travis to want her, but she didn't want to want him. Again, her thoughts seesawed, leaving her more confused than ever. Perhaps she didn't really love Travis at all. Perhaps she just felt a basic biological urge for the first time in her life.

The Tiffany disco was in the basement of the hotel—if you could call a decorator's dream a basement. Dannee carefully made her way down the staircase to the open entrance of the club, halting as she reached the bottom step. The dimmed lights were like pinpricks of light in the roof of a cave and her eyes had not yet adjusted to the darkness. She hesitated to move until she could see where she was going. She had done enough clumsy things these past two days; there was no need to add falling on her face to the list! She took a deep breath, staring through the massive entranceway and into the darkened room. Chattering voices, laughter and music all blended together to make a melodious cacaphony of sound. At least Dannee felt sure that everyone was having a good time.

"As usual, Dannee, you look beautiful. Our table is over here." Travis's voice spoke at her side, warm and reassuring, with almost as much tenderness as the grip on her arm as he led her through the crowd to a comfortable table situated at one corner of the room. There was a definite cooling of the air as they passed the crunch of people and slipped into the dark, padded seats. Travis had known what he was doing when he had chosen this location. It was away from the crush but gave an excellent view of the band and dance floor.

Dannee and a pale Miranda exchanged greetings and Dannee had to admit that Miranda looked super—even when sick, darn her! Her gay personality seemed subdued, however, and suddenly Dannee felt guilty for the wonderful day she had spent with Travis, while Miranda stayed behind, ill.

"Travis tells me the day was perfect for a sail and a picnic." Miranda sighed, leaning over the table to be heard above the loud disco beat. Her hand rested proprietarily on Travis's arm, making Dannee suddenly feel like an intruder. "If I hadn't felt so bad, it would have been nice to join you. As it was, my one wish was to sleep in a comfortable bed until the 'revenge' passed over." She grinned ruefully, her perfect rosebud mouth forming a slight grimace. "But something tells me it's found a home and won't give up that easily."

Dannee stole a look at Travis, but he was watching Miranda sip her drink, her hand still resting on his expensively clothed arm. He looked devastating in a tuxedo—naturally.

"Maybe this will kill the little bugs, or at least make them irritable enough to leave," Miranda murmured.

"You should have stayed in bed, Mandy," Travis said, the concern in his voice echoed in his deep blue eyes.

"And miss all the fun?" she exclaimed. "Why, I've already missed a sailboat ride, a picnic, and a romantic sunset cruise. I should be able to handle this."

Travis covered Miranda's hand with his, giving her a reassuring pat before catching the waiter's eye and ordering a drink for Dannee. Within seconds she had a piña colada in front of her. The waiter gave her a smile as he arranged her cocktail napkin, then disappeared. Dannee sipped the frothy drink, hoping it contained a magic elixir to take away the heavy feeling around her heart which Miranda's obvious closeness to Travis was causing. She glanced up, only to be caught by Travis's glittering eyes. She could feel a flush slowly work its way up her face and hoped the light was poor enough not to show the flags waving in each cheek. Was he thinking of this afternoon, too? As if he could read her mind, he smiled, reaching out to pull her up with him.

"Let's dance," he murmured for her ears alone. "I think I can manage something slow and I need to hold you, so you won't slip away."

Her breath was short and her senses whirled as Travis brought her into the circle of his arms. A slow, Latin beat echoed through the room and her heart beat in rhythm. One of his hands played along the small of her back, molding her to his lean form while the other held her hand against his broad chest, his thumb circling the stone of her ring.

"I'm glad you wore it."

"It's beautiful. Now, I'll always have something special to remind me of Acapulco."

"Aren't beautiful memories enough?" he teased, that incredible smile softening the hard lines of his face. How could she ever have thought he was cold and ruthless?

"Your buying this ring for me is part of a memory."

He was silent as Dannee glanced up at him, knowing her heart was shining in her eyes, and not caring. They stood locked together by invisible bonds and the tension in their bodies communicated the deep need they felt. They stopped dancing, barely swaying to the music, both wrapped in a world of their own.

The tension snapped and, wordlessly, Travis grasped her hand tighter, leading Dannee off the dance floor toward the back of the disco. She followed his lead with such a hammering heart that she could hear a pumping sound in her ears. Dannee didn't care where they were headed, or why. Anything, anything to assuage this feeling.

Two large swinging doors were pushed open and Travis led her through them and down the hall to a small door on the left that turned out to lead to an office.

He guided her in, then closed the door behind them, blocking out the bright overhead hall lights. Travis swung her around, into his arms. In a flash his lips were on hers, searching, seeking, plundering, wreaking havoc with her senses. Strong, yet gentle hands ran up and down her sides, hesitating just below the swell of her breasts, increasing her light-headedness. Dannee clung to him, wanting him more than she had ever wanted anything in her whole life. Her hands pressed against his broad chest, feeling the warm, primitive beat of his quickened heart and reveling in his reaction to her. A coolness hit her warmed skin as Travis expertly unzipped her dress, pulling one side down to expose the roundness of her breast.

"Tempting fruit," he murmured, gently massaging the small bud into a hardened ache. "Tempting little witch."

He turned her against the wall, his weight indelibly pressing his male outline on her. The other offending sleeve was slipped down and she heard a low moan, which she suddenly realized was hers. He took Dannee's hand and placed it inside his shirt, where she could feel his heartbeat, like a triphammer against her palm.

"Feel what you do to me; every time I hold you, see you across the room. First you blow hot and then cold, taunting me, tempting me, flirting, retreating."

His hungry mouth once again claimed hers and bright-colored stars whirled behind her eyelids. She was rocked in his arms before being stretched out on a couch she hadn't even noticed in the darkened room. His hand ran from her hip to her breast, his lips plundering the softness of her slim neck and moving on to nibble at her ear. He was poised above her and the wedge of light coming from under the door allowed her to see the brilliant gleam of his eyes.

He took a deep, shuddering breath, exhaling it slowly, as his palm continued to trace the circle of her hardened nipple. "I want you, Dannee." His voice was quiet and restrained. The look in his eyes told her that he would not make another move until she gave her consent, and frustration welled up in her.

In making her choose, he left her no choice. She couldn't let herself give him what he so obviously wanted—and what she so obviously wanted to give. She covered his hand, removing it from her breast. His other hand brushed aside the tendrils of hair that clung to her forehead as she tried to gather what was left of her pride.

"No."

"I could have gone ahead just now and taken you anyway, but that's not what I want. I want you to admit you want me just as much as I do you." His voice was rasping, showing her as no words could, how much control he was exercising. "What will it take for me to have you?" His question was so low that it took a minute to sink in. When it did, Dannee went rigid. She pushed at his chest as she attempted to sit up.

Travis didn't stop her, just watched her struggle before muttering an imprecation and pulling her up to a standing position. His hands rested on her bare shoulders, then he turned her around and quickly zipped up her dress, straightening the neckline as he did so. He must have had a lot of practice to do it so expertly, Dannee thought derisively.

She glared at him, knowing deep inside that she had welcomed his embrace. She had wanted his touch as she had wanted nothing before, and because of it, he thought she was for sale. Could she blame him for that assumption? Logic told her it was her fault that things had gotten out of hand, but her pride made her blame him.

"You couldn't afford me."

His hands tightened on her shoulders, digging into the pale, coppery skin. "Try me."

They heard the rustle of silk just as the door opened, flooding the room with a bright shaft of light. "Travis? They're getting ready to make the announcement." Miranda stood in the doorway, her face registering the thoughts that must have gone through her mind like wildfire.

Travis never spared a glance for Miranda. His gaze was riveted on Dannee's face. "We'll meet you at the table, Miranda."

When she remained, hesitating, Travis continued, "Why don't you go back to the table? I'll be out with Dannee in a minute. Get out of here; *now*, Miranda."

He didn't raise his voice, but his tone stopped Dannee from fleeing toward the door. Instead, she swung around, giving him a view of her back. Words hung on her lips and were halted by the force of his anger. Dannee heard the door slam, leaving them alone once more.

"I want you, Dannee. You know that," he said quietly, as if Miranda had never interrupted them.

Her chin trembled, then jutted as she faced him. "I want a mountain retreat—a trip around the world—a mink coat. Just because I want them doesn't mean I'll get them any more than you'll get what you want."

"I can give you all those things."

"But I *won't* give you what you want, even if I would like to see you without a penny!"

"You deny you responded to me? To my touch?"

"No." Why lie about the obvious?

His hands reached for, and held hers.

"I can't. I just can't."

A smile slowly crept over his face, a tender smile that was full of the promise of pleasures to come. "I've rushed you. I forget just how young you are. We'll take it easy, one step at a time."

How could he banish her embarrassment so easily, with just the flash of a smile? This was the second time he had put her in an awkward position and then allowed her to get out of it with her dignity, though tattered, still intact.

They walked silently back to the crowded nightclub, Travis's hand on her waist as he guided her through the tables to their seats.

Dannee didn't look at Miranda; she couldn't stand to see the hurt that must be in the other woman's eyes. No one said a word. Miranda twirled her glass, Travis lit a cigarette, and Dannee watched the dancers twirl around the floor. She glanced around the room, wishing desperately for a way to escape, when her eyes lit upon the young man she had seen earlier at the waterfall bar. He smiled in recognition and she returned the smile with more enthusiasm than she meant to, for he immediately stood and began winding his way toward her through the tables.

"May I have this dance?"

Dannee kept her eyes away from Travis's dark frown and grinned at the young man. "Of course," she returned promptly. "That's what a party is for."

She stood and joined him. Her only coherent thought was to get away from the table and try to regain some of her self-esteem.

The music had a fast Latin beat. Tom Leder, as he had introduced himself, had taken lessons and had learned the dance well. He was easy to follow and they both had a good sense of rhythm, doing a twirl during the crescendo of the music, and finishing as he pulled her into his arms and twirled her again. They were both laughing when Dannee felt a tap on her shoulder. Travis took her wordlessly into his arms, dancing her away, leaving Tom standing on the dance floor, empty-handed and dazed. It had happened so quickly that Dannee hadn't had time to protest even if she had wanted to.

"Did you enjoy making a spectacle of yourself with that teenage Don Juan?" Travis muttered between clenched teeth, his hand pressing on the small of her back, holding her much closer than was necessary.

"Yes," she hissed. "More than I enjoyed making a spectacle of myself with you today."

"Which time?" Travis suddenly relaxed his hold, a grin tugging at his mouth. Without waiting for an answer she couldn't come up with, he said, "So that's what it's called. 'Making a spectacle.' I thought we were making love."

"Certainly not! Making love is different. What you were trying to do has nothing to do with love—and that I don't do!"

He laughed aloud, embarrassing her more

than ever. "Why the change of heart now? You didn't seem so offended earlier."

She concentrated on his voice, trying to ignore his hand playing along her spine, moving slowly up and down and keeping her from thinking of anything else.

"I just don't like the role of substitute," she muttered unevenly.

"Good. Because I've never liked substitutes."

"I'm only sorry you needed one today. If all goes well, perhaps Miranda will be well enough tomorrow to take up where I left off."

His eyes narrowed ominously. "What is that crack supposed to mean?"

Suddenly, she was tired of verbal sparring. "Nothing," she mumbled. "I'm sorry. That was uncalled for."

He moved her away so he could see her face, but as he did, the lights brightened. An announcer stood by the microphone welcoming all the contest winners to the party, telling anecdotes about a few of them. Travis and Dannee silently made their way back to the table. Dannee only half listened as Travis pulled out her chair and she sat down.

". . . But all of this wouldn't be possible if it hadn't been for the owner of Travcam Enterprises, owners of Ideal Supermarkets. Without his generosity with the profits from your patronage of his many stores, none of this would have happened. May we hear a warm round of applause for—Mr. Travis Cameron!"

Spotlights swung around, centering on their

table, and on Travis as he smiled and lifted his drink in salute to the crowd. The applause was wild—except for Dannee's.

She stopped in mid-clap, staring at Travis with her mouth open. He glanced at her and grinned, one wicked eyebrow raised.

At that moment she really hated him. He hadn't been kidding when he had said he could give her all those things she had requested in jest. He could afford all that and more! He was even richer than she had ever supposed. Suddenly, what had been bright and strangely promising between them had turned into something cheap and dirty. How many other women had he bought and paid for?

The spotlight was turned off and the music began again. A melodic, jungle beat reverberated through the room.

"Obviously, you're surprised," Travis said, humor tinging his voice.

"Shocked would be more like it." Dannee stood, her trembling hand clutching for her small, silver handbag. "It seems I should have taken you up on your offer, Mr. Cameron. I underestimated your wealth." Her voice shook with anger. "Or perhaps it's better this way. At least I'm not one of a long line."

Miranda looked confused, obviously not quite sure of the direction the conversation had taken. "It wasn't meant to be a shock, Dannee. It was just a pleasant change to meet someone who didn't know who we were or what we were doing here. Most people aren't as nice as you, and make overtures for all the wrong reasons," Miranda explained.

"Oh, how awful for you both," Dannee mockingly sympathized, "but young and naive as I am, I was just the right person to strike up a friendship." She took a deep breath and turned to Travis. "I'm not as discriminating as some, but I promise you, I will be from now on. I have a new meter with which to gauge friendships, you see. It's something along the line of 'money can buy anything—providing one has enough.' Good luck to you both in the future. I have a feeling you're going to need it."

She pivoted and pushed her way through the tables, heading for the stairs, ignoring Travis's voice calling her name. Vaguely, she realized that as she had turned to leave the table, her purse had swung and tilted the bowl of peanuts—right into his lap!

A small sigh of satisfaction passed her lips. Whatever he felt about her, Travis wouldn't soon forget a girl who spent all her time spilling things on him. His cleaning bills would remind him!

Her heart sank to her toes as she turned the key in the lock and walked into the darkened room, not bothering to turn on the lights. He had enough money to pay for any damages she might have cost him, but how could she pay for the hurt *he* had cost *her*? How could she measure the ache that seemed to grow inside her like a snowball rolling downhill?

She threw her purse on the bed and slipped out of her sandals before making her way out to the patio. She didn't notice the tears that rolled down her cheeks while the soft Pacific breeze fanned her blinking eyes.

Two more days and she would be home. . . .

Chapter Ten

Dannee's throat was dry and her eyes ached the next morning when the sun became strong enough to wake her from a restless sleep. She felt drugged and restless. But most of all, she felt hurt.

After last night she would never be able to look Travis in the eye again. All those things she had said about rich men buying young women! And he still had the audacity not only to prove how easy it was to maneuver her into that same situation, but to insist that she would enjoy it too! And worst of all, he had been right. She had allowed him to make love to her, had wanted it with every fiber of her being. If he hadn't asked . . . ! No wonder he had taken for granted his right to what she had, up to now, guarded so carefully.

She remembered the peanuts that had landed in his lap and blushed again, until she thought of his deception. Well—maybe not his deception exactly, but an omission, certainly. He must buy girls all the time and after the way she had acted, why should he have thought she was any different? She moaned aloud and covered her head with the pillow, hiding from the light of day and her own conscience. Oh, how she wished she was home!

The telephone rang, and she reached out, grabbing for it without thought and dragging the receiver to her ear. "Hello?"

"You sound all warm and soft and sleepy." Travis's voice startled her into the present like a cold shower.

"What do you want? To see if I can perform any other cute little tricks?" she asked, bitterly.

"No, the peanuts did very nicely."

"Then why are you calling? Can't you leave me alone?"

"No, I can't. Besides, you don't want me to. Now, get dressed. I'll be up in fifteen minutes and we're going to get a few things cleared up."

"No!"

"You heard me. I'll give you fifteen minutes to get ready."

"Go find Miranda. You're not Superman,

you know. Take care of one girl at a time. Besides, I'm just not your type."

"And just what is my type?"

"Someone who knows the rules to your silly games," she retorted heatedly. "Someone who can be bought as easily as you can buy."

He muttered an expletive.

"I mean it, Travis! Just leave me alone!" She slammed down the receiver.

Tomorrow her vacation would be over and she would resume her life, humdrum as it was. As the years went on, Travis Cameron and Acapulco would seem like a dream. He might be interested in her now, but how would he feel later, when he tired of her? It wouldn't bother him to end the relationship, but she, Dannee, was another story. Dannee knew she loved him too much to risk losing her pride over him, along with everything else. Pride might be the only company she would have in the future, but at least it was something. And it was hers.

She called room service for coffee and toast before heading toward the shower. It was cool and bracing, and made her feel better almost instantly. She stepped out and patted herself dry, determined to fix her mind on something else besides Travis Cameron. This was her vacation and, until yesterday, she had been enjoying it. Her determination stiffened, and she vowed she would enjoy it again. A knock on the door resounded through the room and she wrapped her towel around her, tucking it in to hold it in place.

"Just leave it in the hall," she called through the door, and listened for retreating footsteps.

After a minute or so, she undid the latch and opened the door, looking down at the tiled floor for the tray of coffee she had ordered, but finding instead a pair of highly polished Italian leather shoes—connected to gray, well-tailored slacks—connected to a white knit shirt covering a broad chest and muscled arms.

"You!" she breathed.

Travis stepped in, shutting the door firmly behind him. "I want to talk to you." His deep, blue eyes were icy with anger, his mouth taut with displeasure.

Her chin rose and she glared back at him. "Well, I don't want to talk to you! I told you on the phone, I won't play the game by your rules."

"No, but you'll play by your rules, won't you?" His hands grabbed her arms, his grip tightening as if he wanted to shake her. "You ask for the moon and when I offer it to you, you cry because it's not made of cheese!"

Her teeth dug painfully into her bottom lip. He was right, but he didn't have to throw it in her face! But this was not the time to weaken. "I don't care about *any* games. Just leave me alone! I'm getting dressed now, and when I return I expect you to be gone!"

She turned, stomping toward the closet. As she reached for a simple cotton sundress, her towel unfastened and fell at her feet before she could make a grab for it.

"Am I supposed to go mad with lust now, and tell you how much I want your beautiful little body?"

Her hands couldn't seem to grab the towel fast enough, but when it was once again around her body, she turned and faced him with more pride than dignity. "Yes," she quavered. "And then it's my turn to tell you that I will perish before I give in to *your* brand of lust! Now, *get out!*"

She made what she thought was a grand exit into the bathroom, slamming the door behind her with satisfaction. That man was something else!

She quickly donned the white sundress and sandals. Once again her makeup was sparse, just a touch of lipstick and a little mascara. Acapulco's sun had made sure she needed nothing else. By the time she stepped cautiously out of the bathroom and looked around, she was visibly calmer. There was no sign of Travis. She let out a sigh of relief, refusing to admit that she hadn't expected him to obey her wishes without fuss—or that she hadn't wanted him to.

"The tray is out here, along with your coffee." Travis stood just outside the patio door, a cup of coffee in his hand as he surveyed her, obviously pleased with what he saw and unruffled by her glowering look.

"I see you're still mad," he said calmly,

sipping his coffee. "Come out here and sit down while I try to explain all this to you."

"What?" She smiled sweetly, her venom just barely hidden. "The poor rich man with only one mistress is going to explain base instincts to me? My, how lucky can I get!" She walked slowly toward the patio.

Easy, Dannee, she kept telling herself, don't blow this whole thing out of proportion, or he'll know more than you want him to. "Are two mistresses a status symbol for men like you? Something like Gucci shoes, cashmere sweaters and foreign cigarettes?"

"You jump to the wrong conclusions too quickly, Dannee."

He poured her a cup of coffee, adding cream and sugar, and handed it to her. How could he be so calm? Treating her as if she was a misbehaving child!

"Miranda is not my mistress. But if you want to take that place in my life, as your body tells me you do, then I'd be a fool to turn it down."

"I'd never be your mistress."

"What place do you want in my life, Dannee?" Travis's voice was low with a velvety roughness that underlined his soft words. His eyes gave away the seriousness of his question. She turned away to stare at the trailing bougainvillaea, her heart heavy with unshed tears.

"I haven't asked for a place."

"I want you in my life."

"Why?"

He ignored her question. "Can you say you don't want me?"

She moved her head from side to side, denying his statement, but not the response her body gave as he came up behind her, the length of him touching the length of her, causing a reaction from deep inside.

"No. But that's not enough."

His tense body relaxed and a deep sigh escaped him. "That's what I wanted to hear." He turned her around by her shoulders to face him. His hand took the coffee cup from her, placing it on the low table before pulling her into his arms.

"It may not be enough, but it's a start," he murmured, before his lips closed over hers. She had no choice. She clung to him, their breaths mingling as they kissed, long and deep, trying to satisfy a bottomless need that could only be assuaged in one way.

His hands soothed the burning warmth of her hips and back, awakening other desires, and she pressed herself to him with the same undulating rhythm as the ocean below.

He pulled her arms away from him and took a deep breath. "For a novice, you seem to know all the right moves." He kissed the tip of her nose, letting out a satisfying sigh. "I love it."

"Travis," she hesitated. "What about Miranda?"

"What about her?" His voice sounded distanced, closed, but she plunged ahead anyway.

"Well, I mean, you two seem so close, like—like lovers. And you make such a striking couple."

He chuckled at her last remark before answering, "We are a couple, to some extent. She's been my secretary and right hand for the past three years, and knows almost as much about the business as I do."

"But, the closeness . . ."

"Is just that," he finished for her. "I lean on her to keep me out of the clutches of mothers and their aspiring offspring. When I travel, I don't have to eat alone, or hold up work because my secretary is in an office back home." His voice held a hint of amusement until he saw the look of despair on Dannee's face. Then he turned somber, placing a finger under her chin to raise her eyes to his. "Some things have to be taken on faith, Dannee. My relationship with Miranda is one of the things you have to take my word on, even though it may look different to you and to others. Miranda is *not* my mistress, and that's all that need concern you right now," he said firmly. "But enough on that subject." He gave her a quick squeeze, then glanced at his watch. "You're keeping me from a very important meeting, you know. I should have been there an hour ago." His lips found the curve of her throat and nibbled sensuously. "Will you be waiting for me when I return?"

"When is that?" she asked breathlessly.

"About three o'clock this afternoon. Then, tonight, we're going out on the town."

"I'll be ready," she murmured as their lips met and clung for one last kiss before Travis left.

It never occurred to her until after he was gone that the situation had not changed. He had not really explained anything other than that he and Miranda weren't lovers. Yet, she added to herself, perhaps tonight she could ask him all the questions that kept tumbling through her mind. Questions such as, *would she ever see him again after tomorrow?*

Chapter Eleven

Dannee paced the beach, her heart tumbling over itself as she bounced between happiness and despair. One moment she was ready to do somersaults and the next she was filled with enough doubts to bury her head in the sand. In the short time she had known Travis, she had fallen in love with him, but where was that love leading her? She was afraid to think about marriage, to allow it to enter her head for fear her dreams would be blown away like grains of sand on a windy beach. So now what?

Fate's punishment seemed only fitting. After scoffing at love at first sight for over twenty-two years, she was the victim of that very malady. In a few short days, Travis

Cameron had turned her life upside down.
And the strangest thing of all was that she
wanted to shout her feelings to the world. She
wanted to tell the passersby how much she
loved him. She wanted to write home about
his wondrous smile, his witty sense of humor.
She wanted *everyone* to know how much he
meant to her! Everyone except him. Not yet.
Not until she was sure of his feelings. Her
heart raced at the thought of seeing him this
afternoon. Perhaps by this evening, they
would each know more about the other. . . .

"Miss Hathaway?" A tall, dark-skinned
young man wearing a bellboy's uniform ap-
proached, his eyes gleaming in appreciation
of her lithe, supple body and ready smile.

"Yes?"

"This is for you." He handed her an envelope stamped with the hotel emblem, and her
heart began racing faster than ever. She dug
in her purse for change and held out a handful
of coins to him, smiling.

"Thank you!" he cried, eyes gleaming, and
Dannee knew she must have over-tipped
again.

Dannee ripped the envelope apart in her
hurry, barely allowing the message to remain
intact. Her breath caught in her throat as she
glanced down at the signature. It was signed
Miranda, and for a fleeting moment she was
tempted to fold it back up and deliver the crisp
paper to the sea.

Nonsense! There was no reason for her to
have a guilty conscience about Miranda.

Hadn't Travis explained to her about their relationship? She glanced down at the scrawled message.

"Dannee, please come to my hotel room, #554. I need to ask you a favor.

Thanks,
Miranda"

Dannee turned, retracing her steps back to the hotel, her feet visibly dragging all the way. Everything was too new, and too much was happening for her to absorb all the events and emotions. It was odd to think that she had been in Acapulco for only five days, yet it seemed like five years. What was Miranda going to say? And why had she summoned Dannee now?

When she finally stood in front of Miranda's door, she knocked louder than she had intended, and almost startled herself with the noise.

"Come in," a feeble voice called.

Dannee turned the knob and walked in.

Miranda stood in front of the closet door, one hand gripping the edge of the jamb as she glanced over her shoulder at Dannee. "I'm so glad you came." She smiled wanly, her lids drooping, her face white with the effort of standing. She was still ill, and if looks were anything to go by, feeling worse than yesterday.

Dannee hurried to her side and walked her

to the edge of the bed, helping her to sit down. "You shouldn't be up and around, Miranda. You should be in bed, seeing a doctor," she exclaimed worriedly. She reached for the telephone, only to stop with her hand in midair at Miranda's words.

"The doctor just left," she said tiredly, resting her head against the back of the bed.

"What did he say?"

"He told me to catch the next plane home and see my family physician." She gave another small smile. "He seemed to think that the flu bug wasn't my only problem, and that I must be run down." Miranda stared at the lifeless hands in her lap as if they belonged to someone else.

Miranda glanced up at Dannee. "I'm leaving on the five o'clock plane tonight." She waved one limp hand, as if to brush away a fly. "But that's not why I asked you here. Yesterday you said that you had taken your two week vacation in order to go on this trip, right?"

Dannee's confused eyes met Miranda's as she nodded her head and wondered where all this was leading.

"And you also said that you really loved Acapulco and wished you could stay for a little while longer, right?"

Dannee's confusion grew. All this was true, but where were Miranda's questions leading?

"And if I go home, Travis will be without a secretary, right?"

Suddenly it all came clear in Dannee's

mind. "And you want me to take your place?" she asked incredulously?

"Why not? It's the perfect solution. I have to go home to recuperate before the wedding and you *are* a secretary. What better way to stay in Acapulco than to be Travis's secretary for the next five or six days. You'll get time off to see the sights and even get paid for it!"

Miranda's hand trembled as she reached for Dannee's, her blond hair glistening in the sunlight like the tears in her eyes. "With you here, I know Travis will be safe from all the grasping, grabbing females lying in wait for a husband."

"You're getting married?" Dannee croaked, her thoughts still on Miranda's first statement.

Miranda smiled, her tears threatening to spill over. "Yes, I finally talked him into it." She held out her hand to show Dannee a large emerald cut diamond sitting on a white gold band. "We've been hesitating for over a year now, because of upsetting personal circumstances. But after talking to Travis yesterday, we've decided to go ahead and do it."

She looked at Dannee, love bringing a slight bloom to her pale face. "I can't tell you how much of a relief it is to finally make that decision. I've been on the fence for a year, but now I know I'm doing the right thing. I know it."

Miranda leaned back, totally spent. She closed her eyes for a moment, before continuing. "Travis has to close this deal before next week, when he meets me in San Francisco. Without a secretary, that would be impossible. And he likes you, Dannee, I know it."

Dannee stared at Miranda, terrified of the deep emotions that surged through her.

"Why, he said only last night that he thought you were a very nice girl and that you probably did your job very dependably."

"When?" Dannee croaked.

"Right after you spilled the peanuts in his lap." Miranda gave a small giggle, holding her stomach with one hand, as if it hurt to laugh.

It hurt Dannee, too. Her own world was falling down around her in pieces. He had been making fun of her behind her back! That lying, two-timing, arrogant . . . ! No, he hadn't lied about Miranda. She *wasn't* his mistress—she was his fiancée!

"Please, Dannee?" Miranda pleaded. "Even after I get well, I've still got so much to do for the wedding that I won't be able to return to work."

"If you think for one minute that I would work for the great Travis Cameron, you're wrong! I wouldn't lift him out of a mudhole!" Dannee's anger finally erupted and in so doing, her voice reached an echoing pitch.

"Trying to do the impossible again, Miranda?" a silky, male voice inquired, and Dannee whirled around. Her hands formed into fists that would dearly have loved to strike Travis but instead dropped impotently to her sides.

He stood in a doorway that Dannee hadn't noticed before, one that apparently connected Miranda's room with the room next door. His shirt was unbuttoned and hung loosely from his shoulders, displaying a mat of dark, springy hair on his virile chest. His eyes held hers for a moment before turning back to Miranda, but the puzzlement he showed didn't register with Dannee, so furious was she.

"Dannee wouldn't be able to help you to the car, much less take your place with the paperwork." Travis's eyes raked Dannee's figure, only to return to her face, almost laughing at her impotent anger.

"How sweet! And you even have adjoining rooms!" Dannee smiled, wishing her teeth could break the skin on his corded neck. "And am I supposed to move in here?" she asked Miranda, fighting to keep her smile in place.

"They're adjoining rooms, with an extra room off Travis's that we use as an office, so it would probably be easier if you did," Miranda ignored Dannee's sarcasm and answered, her voice hopeful. "Does that mean you'll do it?"

Dannee stared at them both. She wanted to scream "No! Never!" at them, but the words wouldn't make it past the lump in her throat.

"The room is yours." Travis bowed, extending his hand mockingly, as if he held a silver platter. "I must say, it will be quite different from the way I expected to wind up my business vacation."

"Yes, it will, won't it?" Dannee's words hit

her mark, and as proof, Travis's eyes glittered and a tautness became visible around his mouth.

"Are you sure you're grown up enough for the job? Most adults realize that certain things have to be taken on faith, but it's obvious you haven't reached that point yet." His voice was soft, menacing, and something else. Sad? No, it couldn't be. The only thing he could have to be sad about was being found out!

"Only the gullible take things on faith, Mr. Cameron. I was taught by a pro and believe me, I will never be gullible again," Dannee said, with every ounce of dignity she could muster.

"Please, don't let Travis's teasing upset you, Dannee." Miranda held one pale hand to her head as if the words made it ache. Only it wasn't Miranda whose head was aching, it was Dannee. "Travis is always tense before signing contracts, and this one has been the very devil." Miranda stood, swaying, and Travis was instantly at her side. He held her gently, leading her to a large, overstuffed chair next to the outside door.

"Stay here," he ordered her, his business-like mask now in evidence. "Let me change my shirt and I'll take you to the airport."

He disappeared through the connecting door, shutting it firmly behind him as if to shut Dannee out.

Anger such as she'd never felt before surged through her, and without thinking, she pulled the door open and walked into Travis's room, slamming the door behind her with a resounding bang. Her momentum continued until she stood in front of him. Then she became suddenly embarrassed. He was standing by the closet, his shirt off to show the dark, even tan on his broad back and shoulders. When he turned to acknowledge her, his eyes questioned her motives with a condescending look.

"Do you want something?"

"Yes! I want to tell you just what I think of you, Mr. Travis Cameron the Great!" she whispered loudly, keeping herself from shouting when she remembered Miranda in the next room.

"Go ahead, I'm listening," he answered calmly, undoing the buckle at his waist and completely disconcerting Dannee. She forgot the words she had wanted to say, so flustered was she. Her hand covered his, not wanting to see him in any greater a state of undress than he was in at this moment.

"Don't!" she protested, stilling his hand. He turned his palm up and captured hers.

"Don't what? Don't stop? Don't undress? Don't be angry? Don't leave? I'm never sure what you mean, Dannee. You say one thing, not very clearly, then act in a way that conflicts with whatever you've just said."

"Don't undress. What did you think I meant?" she asked, attempting to find the impetus her anger had given her. It had brought her this far, only to desert her now.

"There's only one way to stop that sharp

tongue of yours, Dannee," Travis muttered, as his hand snapped her off balance and into his arms. "You're a little wildcat, and I'll be hung if I can understand why."

Before she could tell him, his lips covered hers in a brutal kiss, silencing all the words that tumbled about inside her brain. His touch was like an intoxicating drug, and even the roughness of it did not deflect Dannee from the sheer enjoyment of being held close to his lean, hard body. His hands dug into her slim waist, holding her close to his hips as his tongue ravaged her tender mouth. She was both excited and frightened, and one emotion fought with the other for supremacy. Fright won, and Dannee struck out at him, her small fist beating against his back as she struggled for breath.

Travis dropped his arms immediately, and if it had not been for his grip on her elbow, Dannee would have fallen. She stared up at him, eyes as wide as soft, brown saucers.

"I'll keep that remedy in mind the next time your tongue runs away with you." He turned, slipping a clean white shirt off a hanger and onto his shoulders, methodically buttoning it across his dark-haired chest.

"The next time my tongue runs away, you won't be anywhere around to use that remedy!" Dannee ran toward the door, her mission forgotten in the humiliation of his kiss. All she could do was run, and run she did, right into the next room—where she came face to face with Miranda.

She took a deep breath, hoping the red flags in her cheeks would subside before the other girl noticed. And she didn't; she was apparently feeling much too ill to notice anything short of an earthquake, Dannee thought. Miranda apparently thought she had followed Travis merely to finalize their arrangements for the job, as her words made clear.

"Thank you, Dannee. I feel much better now, knowing Travis is in your hands," Miranda said simply, bowing her head as if she was too tired to look up.

"Is there anything I should know?" Dannee questioned resignedly.

While Dannee quickly finished Miranda's packing for her, they discussed the business deal Travis was working on. A string of modern convenience supermarkets was about to be built and Travis would be involved with building them and supplying the foodstuffs they needed to open.

When Dannee had folded and packed Miranda's clothes and closed the suitcase, she sat on the edge of the bed, only half listening to Miranda go into the myriad details of the job.

Only one thing was certain; Travis really was here on business. It was probably the only thing he had said that was true. All that hullabaloo about Miranda being only a friend had been just that. He had lied to her, and the anger she had felt only minutes ago disappeared, curling into a small ball of agony somewhere in the region of her heart.

Why had she been stupid enough to accept this job? Why hadn't she run?

The only reason she could rationally give herself was that she wanted to show him just how good she was at her job. No more clumsiness. She'd show him what a really valuable secretary was!

But somehow, that thought didn't take away the hurt.

Chapter Twelve

Dannee's fingers were ready to form callouses on top of callouses. She switched off the electric typewriter and leaned back in the swivel chair, rubbing the small of her back. Her back was cramped, her fingers were sore, her eyes were blurred and her heart ached. And right now, she couldn't even put her pains in order of importance. She just knew she was miserable, and had been ever since Miranda had left, four days ago. They had been four very long days, she realized, as she thought back over them.

When Travis had returned after driving Miranda to the airport, he had gone straight to Dannee's room, only to find her packing. "Are you that eager to move into Miranda's room?"

he had questioned, one eyebrow rising in mock amusement as he sauntered past her and toward the open suitcase lying on the bed, half-filled with clothes that were more wadded than folded.

"I thought that was what you wanted? I thought you just couldn't wait?" Dannee's anger showed itself in more than her tone as she slammed the door and walked to the low dresser to empty the last drawer. She found the shirt he had given her, still in its wrapping, and the sight of it made her angrier than ever. She vowed to herself that she would never wear it.

"Just what is it you've been accusing me of all afternoon, Dannee? I came in from a business appointment, eager to see the girl of my dreams, and all I hear is my name taken in vain." He shook his head and tut-tutted, his composure making her even more angry.

"You came in here this morning and sweet-talked me like the smooth-talking hustler that you are, and I was stupid enough to buy it. That's what makes me mad! All the time you were making passes at me, you had Miranda in the next room, wearing an engagement ring that could pass as a paperweight for the entire U.N.!"

Dannee threw the rest of her belongings in the suitcase, too busy being angry to notice Travis's rage until she closed the lid of the suitcase with a snap and glanced up. When she did, a gasp escaped her lips, and she waited for his inevitable retaliation.

Somehow, he kept himself under rigid control. He stood just two feet from her, his hands on his hips as his steely blue-gray eyes bored through her, pinning her in place. Every nerve in her body screamed with tension brought on by his closeness to her, but still she couldn't move. The silence stretched until she could hardly bear it, but she was afraid to break the spell and unleash the anger that seemed to be pointed directly at her like a loaded gun.

"Jealous?"

His question broke the spell. "Jealousy has nothing to do with it," she snapped, throwing her comb into her open purse. "I just can't stand rich men like you, men who believe the world is theirs for the buying. You bought Miranda, and now you think you can buy me." She snapped her purse shut. "It's disgusting!"

"I haven't bought you yet, Dannee." His insolent gaze raked her slim body from head to foot. "But I will. Are you asking for another offer?"

She needed an outlet for her anger and, without thinking, she raised her hand and prepared to strike. But she was too slow, for Travis grabbed her wrist, twisting it behind her as he pulled her toward his lean, hard body.

"Are you trying to goad me, Dannee? Or don't you know what you're doing?"

Dannee's eyes spit fire as she clamped her mouth shut.

"I see. You *don't* know what you're doing."

147

His anger disappeared, to be replaced by grim humor.

"Yes I do. I'm leaving. I don't have to take anything from you!"

"No, you're not leaving. You promised Miranda you would help out, and you're going to do just that. Right after you explain to me what happened between this morning and this afternoon to make you hate me so."

"I don't believe it!" She stared at him in amazement, her anger feeding on her frustration. She couldn't believe that he didn't know what he had done, and there was certainly no way to tell him without humiliating herself further. Well, she would have to try. "You came into my bedroom this morning, made love to me, gave me a song and dance about Miranda, then walked out feeling smug about the way you had hoodwinked me! There was only one problem—you forgot that Miranda can talk too. She told me all about going home so she can get ready for the wedding. *And* how you're meeting her in San Francisco."

"I see," he murmured. His eyes focused on Dannee, as if to read her soul. But all that was visible was anger and indignation. "And instead of asking me for an explanation, you jumped to conclusions, not only dirtying my reputation, but blemishing Miranda's as well by implying that her duties were more than merely secretarial. That she can't separate business from pleasure, as it were."

"How astute of you!"

"And you really believe it?" His hands

tightened on her wrists. Suddenly, he released her, throwing her hands from him and walking across the room as if he could no longer control his actions. "Very well. Let's say you're right. I apologize for making a pass at you. I didn't realize just how young and inexperienced you are." His voice was taut and controlled.

What was he so mad about anyway? That he had been caught? Dannee's mind was whirling in confused thought.

"Now that you've found me out, you'll know better how to handle me, and I'll know I can't play around with the hired help."

He turned and stared out the patio doors. "With that understanding between us, we should be able to work together well. I still need a secretary for the next six days. Do you still want to stay in Acapulco? My work will probably take five or six hours of your time daily. That still leaves you plenty of time for sightseeing."

Dannee stared at his rigid back. The sting of tears was in her eyes. No! She wanted to scream. I want you to hold me—to love me—to tell me that Miranda means nothing to you, and that I mean everything!

But her common sense forced words to her lips and though she almost told him where he could spend the wintry days, somehow the exact opposite came tumbling out. . . .

"I'll take the job as long as you realize that that's exactly what it is, a *job*. Any funny business and I'll leave immediately."

"That's fine with me." He turned, his face blank and voice cleansed of all emotion. "You can move into Miranda's room, not because it adjoins mine, but because it's easier for me to work when you're nearby and because the typewriter and files are already set up. I'll see you at nine tomorrow morning. Be ready to work."

He walked to the door, his hand on the knob before stopping. "By the way, no one is so irresistible that she could arouse my 'male lust' beyond control. But if it would make you feel better, there's a lock on the door. For your naive peace of mind, use it."

Humiliated as it made her feel, she did.

Dannee worked virtually alone for the first two days. She organized the files and familiarized herself with the many briefs and plans, as per Travis's instructions in the notes he left every morning before she arrived. The contracts were full of long and drawn out legal terminology, but she muddled through them somehow. She had even begun to understand the ins and outs of opening a chain of stores in Mexico versus the United States, and had unwillingly grown a grudging respect for Travis's business acumen. It was not the easiest business venture to pull off, and many men would not have been capable of it.

Dannee stretched her cramped fingers that second afternoon before placing the cover on the typewriter to signal the end of the day.

The small, compact model was a delight to use compared to the large, cumbersome machine she had at home. Home. It seemed so far away from her now. It was hard to imagine going back and becoming a part of that life again after having been to Acapulco—and having known Travis.

She sighed, walking slowly toward her room, just as the door opposite her swung open. Travis stood in the doorway, a drink in his hand, his tie loosened to hang down in front of him like a scarf. The top button of his shirt was undone, and she noticed the dark hairs curling there. She watched as his eyes focused on the desk, then glanced around the room to fix on Dannee.

A small smile tugged ruefully at his mouth, and her heart lurched. He lifted his glass to her in mock salute. "Have a drink? I'm glad I caught you; I've got a few things to discuss."

Dannee's eyes widened, questioning his invitation.

He clarified. "You might as well stick around. I'm in no mood to write long business letters to you just so you can write long business letters to my associates."

Dannee nodded, irritated that she couldn't trust her voice. She couldn't think of anything to say. She reluctantly pulled away from the nice, secure handle of her bedroom door and walked cautiously to the small couch, perching on the edge like some small mouse poised to flee.

151

Travis turned abruptly and left the room, retracing his steps to the small, portable bar in his own room.

Dannee could see his broad back and hear the clink of glasses as he mixed her drink. What was he serving her? Whatever it was, she would take only a sip, just to be sociable. Alcohol made people talk, and that she wouldn't do. She had made up her mind on that score ever since she had taken this job. Never, never would she allow him to know how much she cared. And drinking wasn't conducive to keeping secrets any more than her uninhibited responses to his kisses had been.

"Here you go," he said softly, handing her a frosty drink before sitting down next to her. She edged closer to the arm of the couch but he was oblivious to her withdrawal. He leaned his head back to rest on the rim of the couch and closed his eyes, expelling his breath with a weary sigh.

"Let's hope I haven't loused this deal up too badly, Dannee. *Señor* Martinez drives a hard bargain, and I don't think I can give any more concessions than I already have."

Dannee sipped her drink, trying to decide just how much liquor Travis had put into it, but she didn't have enough experience to judge. However, his words were putting her at ease. Business was really his big problem. Her heart warmed and she almost felt sorry for him until she remembered a few of the female voices on the telephone these past two days.

She turned her attention back to the present. "What do you mean? Can he call off the entire negotiations?" she questioned.

"He can," Travis answered, running a hand around his neck and lifting his head to take another sip before resuming his original position. "But I don't think he will. Not now."

"What's so special about now?"

"The negotiations are too far along. He's just giving me a hard time because he wants the best deal he can get. I don't blame him, but neither am I willing to come out of this without something to show."

"Is he trying that hard? The contract I just typed up, the one concerning the importation of canned goods, seemed fair to both sides." Dannee's brow furrowed as she tried to remember the exact wording of the first full contracts she had typed, which was hard, because she was just beginning to understand the foreign language of the law.

"No," Travis mumbled, "it was fair. But now he's trying to get to me on floor space." His eyes opened to show a flash of anger. "But there's no point and no profit in building any smaller. Any less square footage and you'll crowd the display space. This is supposed to be a modern supermarket, not a family food-store!"

His hand reached for hers, and she gave a comforting squeeze. Suddenly, all his problems with the negotiations faded as they both remembered other times when their hands had touched, just like this.

He smiled at her, his eyes warm with soft laughter. "Drink up, Dannee."

She sipped obediently.

He sighed. "I'm sorry for taking my frustrations out on you, but you're such a good listener."

He sounded so much like a little boy, he suddenly brought out her protective instincts. It was as if he had been hurt and turned to her for a kiss to make it better. The impression was so strong that she leaned over without thinking and gave him a soft kiss on the lips to help soothe away his imaginary battle scars.

"Ummmm, that's nice. Do it here." He pointed to his temple, and she gave him another kiss.

"Is that better?" she teased breathlessly, unwilling to spoil this gentle moment between them.

"Much. Now kiss me here," he said drowsily, leaning his head back as he pointed to his other temple.

Dannee leaned forward to better position herself on the couch, her knees drawn up beneath her. Travis smiled, and she saw the small lines around his eyes that the sun and laughter had made. They only made him more attractive.

"You're beautiful," he growled, his arms

coming around her to pull her into his lap. "Absolutely beautiful." His lips teased the side of her neck, leaving a trail of fire in their wake. He pulled back to look at her through half closed eyes before lightly touching his lips to hers, gently teasing hers apart before pulling away just out of reach. "Maybe the most beautiful woman I've ever seen."

"Is that right?" she breathed, and he nodded.

His lips were poised bare millimeters from hers; she could feel his warm breath teasing her mouth as he spoke. She closed her eyes, loving this sweet torment, wanting to feel his lips pressed on hers with the full measure of his longing, yet not wanting to see this moment end. While his lips tortured hers with their nearness, his hands moved slowly along her body. He molded her tiny waist between his palms and then his hands slid upward, pressing her ribs before coming to rest just below the gentle swell of her breasts.

She drew her breath in slowly and tilted her head slightly to bring her lips into contact with his. He immediately took command, deepening the kiss and tasting her to the fullest while his long, sensitive fingers teased her breasts and made her moan with longing. She arched herself against him, fitting her curves more fully to his strength, and she heard his breath rasp harshly in his throat as he whispered her name against her lips.

"Oh, Dannee," he breathed huskily, "you

don't know what you do to me. We have to stop this; you don't know what you're letting yourself in for."

But she was beyond rational thought now and no more capable of drawing the sweet, lingering kiss to a close than he was. She answered him only by teasing his lips with hers and, with a groan, he tightened his embrace and lowered his head to the shadowed valley between her breasts. He pushed the soft fabric of her top aside and stopped to gaze at the naked beauty before him. Then he buried his hands in her gleaming hair and gently took her firm breast in his mouth to tease the rosy peak to hardness with his tongue.

Dannee gasped aloud with pleasure. No man had ever made her feel as Travis made her feel. She knew this was wrong; she tried to think of Miranda, but she was in the grip of passions whose strength she had yet to fathom and she could only twine her fingers through Travis's thick black hair and press him closer to her.

He stopped and pulled away from her slightly, and she felt the chill of the air where his warm and compelling mouth had been only moments before. "I'm glad you're here, Dannee. I want you to be here—loving me."

"And am I—loving you?" she questioned in an innocently provocative tone, too bemused to know what she was saying.

"You will be in a minute." His arms tightened and their lips melded together once more as he slowly drugged her into a state of complete lethargy.

Her hand rubbed against the springy hair of his chest, loving the feel of his hardened muscles as the hairs tickled her palm. He was caressing her slowly, all over, and nothing had ever felt this good.

He twisted Dannee around slowly until her back was on the couch and his weight was on her, where it belonged. His hands soothed her, finding nerve endings she never knew she had. The male scent of him filled her nostrils, adding to the overpowering sensations flooding her.

She lost all track of where she was. She thought she could feel the warmth of the sun breathing down on her; waves could have been splashing at their feet, the sand grainy against her back, just like the nubs of the couch. Couch! Her senses suddenly returned and humiliation flooded through her as she realized what she was doing with a man who would soon be marrying another.

Dannee's eyes flashed open to see Travis above her, and she pushed hard against him, taking him unaware and knocking him to the floor.

"Oh, no, not again!" she yelled breathlessly. "Not ever again, Mr. 'Love 'em and Leave 'em' Cameron! You made a fool out of me once, but you'll never have the opportunity to do it again!"

His expression of surprise turned quickly to anger that deepened with an intensity Dannee didn't know how to fend off. His breathing was irregular, the only sound in the otherwise quiet room. "You liked it the first time, Dannee. You didn't even fight me off that night in the office. What's so different about now?" His voice was calm, questioning.

His voice was so conversational in tone, yet he lay sprawled on the floor, one elbow propping him up. The funny side of it struck Dannee and she began to giggle. Her giggles turned into laughter, and her laughter turned into hysteria.

"Dannee! Stop it!" Travis ordered, sitting down next to her again, his hands shaking her by the shoulders to bring her back to sanity.

Dannee couldn't seem to stop the tears rolling down her cheeks, hard as she tried. By the time she was able to get control of herself, her first thought was to preserve her pride in front of Travis. She must never let him see how she felt, how deeply hurt she was inside.

"Well, don't let anyone tell you that you don't have a marvelous sense of the ridiculous, Travis. You've just made my day!"

"What do you mean?"

"I mean," she said, wiping her eyes with the corner of her blouse, "that you looked absolutely ridiculous sitting in the middle of the floor with surprise written all over your face! You could have posed for Humpty-Dumpty when he hit the earth!"

"I see," he said through clenched teeth. "So once again, the unicorn falls prey to the maiden." He stood, reaching for his half-finished drink. "Now that I've provided some amusement for you, I think I'll retire and lick my wounds in private."

The telephone jangled in the silence, and Travis bent to pick it up, barking into the receiver, "Yes, what is it?"

His voice changed instantly, turning warm, and intimate. . . . "I was just thinking of you, and how lovely you looked last night in the moonlight," he murmured, just loud enough for Dannee to hear. "Are you willing to repeat the evening with me? Say around nine-thirty? Fine, I'll take you to Chico and Charlie's." He hesitated, listening to the voice on the other end. His glance centered on Dannee, sitting wide-eyed on the couch and he smiled coldly.

"Yes, darling. I feel the same way." He spoke softly, but Dannee reacted to his loving words, spoken to another woman, like a slap in the face. She stood on trembling legs and almost stumbled as she made her way to her own door, slamming it with a vengeance.

This game was too much for her. She couldn't understand his rules and only got herself in deeper trouble every time she tried to play. And it was all her own fault, a little voice prodded. Dannee ignored it. All that little voice had ever done was to tell her too late about trouble. Besides, she was hurt enough without having subconscious recriminations tossed down on her head along with everything else!

She made a resolution. Two could play his game, no matter how much it hurt. From now on she would be cool and complacent around him, just as he had been around her these past few days. What was sauce for the goose was sauce for the gander, too, and she intended to prove it.

Now, two days after that last scene, Dannee ran her hands through her hair, rubbing the back of her neck to help relieve tension. She had been typing since early that morning, and now, as she glanced through the window, she realized the sun would be setting soon, beginning its nightly show. It reminded her of how drastically things had changed since the evening Travis had taken her on the cruise.

Now, he ignored her or treated her with barely veiled hostility, talking curtly in as few words as possible unless he was dictating letters.

She never knew where he was when he wasn't with her. With that other woman, she supposed. Poor Miranda! Did she really have any idea of what she was getting into? All Dannee knew anymore was that her body felt like one big bruise and it wasn't due to the work. It was due to Travis. All her life, Dannee had scoffed at love, laughed at those who succumbed to it. And now, here she was, in the very predicament she had always mocked. All she could think of now was Travis and Miranda, together. His hands touching her, his lips caressing that beautiful skin, the children they would have, children with dark hair and startling blue eyes. His—stop it! she commanded herself.

She swept back her hair, allowing the breeze to cool the nape of her slender neck, and was startled when the door to the suite opened. Her breath caught in her throat and she looked quickly away, not wanting Travis to see the pain in her eyes as he stood there with a dark-eyed beauty. His arm was draped casually around her waist as he walked her toward Dannee's desk.

"Dannee, I'd like you to meet *Señorita* Teresa Martinez. Teresa, my secretary, Dannee Hathaway."

The Latin woman's eyes moved casually over Dannee's form, taking in the jeans and short, knit top that casually molded Dannee's figure.

"You've heard me speak of her father," Travis went on. "He's the gentleman who's been liaison for the government."

"How do you do, *Señorita* Martinez." Dannee shook the woman's hand, deliberately pumping the limp wrist. What had the lady expected, a kiss on those perfectly manicured fingers? Dannee ignored the warning signs flashing from Travis's eyes as she stood and stretched, tightening the material that was already snug against her breasts.

"I was just about to take a break. Would you like me to leave?" she asked innocently, unable to mistake the cold anger that had entered Travis's eyes.

"That might be a very good idea, Dannee. After a short walk, you might not make as many mistakes."

Darn him! He had noticed the eraser next to her typewriter, an eraser which was decidedly smaller than it had been this morning.

She walked across the room to the door, only looking back as her hand reached for the knob. "Would you like me to have coffee sent up?"

"I think we can manage on our own," Travis answered dryly, his eyes now glued to the woman beside him, who smiled up at him as if he were her entire world. She had tucked one hand into his arm and was holding on as if she couldn't keep her balance any other way, while the other reached up and smoothed, in a seductive fashion, the lapel of his dark gray suit.

Dannee didn't realize she was staring until Travis glanced up, crooking an eyebrow as if to ask what she wanted. She was obviously a fifth wheel. Blushing, she turned, almost yanking the knob off the door.

"Oh, and Dannee?"

Dannee pivoted again, her face mutinous.

"Don't spill anything, will you?"

Color rushing to her cheeks, she left, slamming the door with a resounding bang!

It took her over an hour to calm down enough to go back to her room. She had walked along the beach, mumbling speeches she would love to make to that pompous, self-righteous, arrogant man! The only problem was, she knew she would never give them. She should have made them four days ago, but it was too late now. She should also have gone home when her original five days were over, but that, too, was hindsight. Now she was embroiled in an emotional mess that controlled her thoughts night and day, and she didn't see any way to escape, even by leaving Acapulco.

The only fact that Dannee was certain of was that the pain of leaving Travis in two days time would be worse than the pain of staying with him. She remembered that morning in her room—that day Miranda left— and a warm glow of feeling blocked out the anger she had felt only moments before. She should have let him make love to her. At least then she would have the memory of that one magic interlude to take with her through life.

She slowly opened the suite door, her head bent and shoulders drooping. It would do her no good at all to rehash the scene she had just witnessed between the beautiful, dark-haired *Señorita* Martinez and Travis. She had already tortured herself enough thinking about him with Miranda, did she have to go through that again, imagining a different woman in his arms? She must be mad!

"Where on earth have you been?" Travis's angry voice echoed across the room, startling her.

"I went for a walk. Didn't I give you enough time?"

She controlled the urge to glance around

the room. She wasn't going to look at *Señorita* Teresa Martinez if she could help it. Travis stood by the window. The late afternoon light flooding around him formed wicked shadows on his handsome face.

"Plenty!" he bit out. "Enough time to seduce *three* women!"

Dannee grinned in spite of herself. So the lady in question was gone!

Travis took a few steps toward her, but she stood her ground. If she was going to fight the attraction she felt for him, she might as well start now! But her knees and hands apparently hadn't received her silent command, for they began their usual shaking, just as they always did when Travis stood too close.

"My, aren't we energetic." She smiled, sweetly. "Would you like me to recruit a few more ladies for you, or can you handle it by yourself?"

Travis's hands came down on her shoulders and grasped her tightly. "I should punish you for that last remark." His hands tightened their grip, and his eyes narrowed with anger.

She stared up at him, refusing to flinch at the raw anger that flowed from him. He was hurting her, but she refused to give in to the pain. After all, it took her mind off the pain she had been living with for four days now.

His dark blue eyes focused on her slightly parted lips, and his hands slowly loosened their grip to softly stroke the red marks his fingers had made on her skin. It was a slow, sensuous caress, more punishing than his taut fingers had been, though in an entirely different way.

Her eyes widened as she watched his anger melt, and the soft contours of her mouth formed a small "o" as she realized his intention.

"Oh, Dannee," he murmured, bringing his mouth down to hers with tantalizing slowness.

Dannee couldn't move. She was mesmerized, as if swaying to the music of a swami's flute. Travis's lips covered hers, bringing her blood to the boiling point. She tried to ignore his hypnotic hold on her, but it was to no avail. She could hardly breathe. She closed her eyes in heady release. This was what she had wanted all along. She wanted to be the one in his arms. She wanted to be kissed to distraction. She wanted . . .

Her arms closed about his neck. She drew him closer to her, loving the rough texture of his slacks against her bare, tanned legs. Her breasts pressed against his hard chest, and her heart beat in unison with his.

Her hands traveled through his hair, feeling the springy texture under her fingertips before they wandered over his shoulders and neck to rest on either side of his strong jaw. Her actions were proving her feelings for him, once and for all. All that mattered was now, this moment, this kiss . . . . His lips came up, trailing kisses along her forehead and cheeks.

"I should punish you even more," he whispered hoarsely, and his hands traveled down her body, sending new passion shooting through her. His touch gave her sustenance, and she could no more stop the moan that rose from deep in her throat than she could stop her hands from wandering over his hard chest and corded arms.

His hands roamed over the thin material of her shorts to pull her against him so that there was only the fabric to keep them apart. His other hand slid beneath her shirt where it cupped and teased a breast, his thumb flicking over a rosy-tipped nipple to send sparks coursing through her, and as his lips once more claimed hers, she gave him back, measure for measure, the passion he was showing her. There was no stopping now. She wanted him so badly that nothing else mattered. Her response was complete, and she told him so in every movement of her body. She was a dying woman—and only his touch could give her life. . . .

His hands came up and drew her arms away from him as he took a step back. His breath was as erratic as hers, but she didn't notice it. She wanted to be back with him, and her confused look confirmed the fact.

"Your offer is mighty tempting. Too tempting for me to take you up on. You're not prepared to live with the consequences of your action right now," he said quietly.

If cold water had been dashed on Dannee, she couldn't have been more rudely awakened. "I haven't offered you a thing!"

"Then what was that little display about

just now? If you weren't finally prepared to give me what I had asked for earlier, what were you up to?" he asked, calmly.

"I—it—none of your business!" She spun quickly around, not wanting him to see the tears in her eyes. Once again, she had made a complete fool of herself, and they both knew it!

"Someday I'm going to take you up on that offer, but right now, I have to attend to some business."

"Yes, sir!" she bit out sarcastically. "Is that all for today, sir? Have you had your quota of girls for the day, sir?"

"Watch it, Dannee! I'm on a short leash right now, and given enough provocation, might decide to take you up on what you were offering just a moment ago, with—or without—your permission!"

He glanced impatiently at his watch. "It's six-thirty now. *Señor* Martinez is giving a business party tonight. Be ready at eight o'clock, sharp."

"You've got to be kidding!"

He shook his head, eyes narrowed. "Oh, no. I'm not kidding," he said ominously.

"I'm not going!"

"Yes you are. It's part of the job."

Her temper flared, the fire of passion now turned into unreasonable anger. "Oh, no! My job ends when I leave the typewriter!"

"Then take it with you." Travis turned and walked toward his door. With his hand on the knob, he faced her again. "Your job also ends when you get paid—and that won't happen if you don't attend this party!" He opened the door. "Be ready."

The door closed softly behind him, saying more with its silence than if he had slammed it.

Dannee stood uncertainly in the center of the room. She was still trembling from reaction, but which reaction, she didn't know. Until she had met Travis, she had honestly believed herself to be a normal girl with normal emotions. Now she knew she was wanton, nervous, excitable—and crazy! No matter how he treated her, she loved him. What could the evening have in store for her that could be any worse than what she had already gone through today?

Chapter Thirteen

They drove slowly along the cliff road. Travis's hands were steady on the wheel of the Mercedes as he negotiated the hairpin curves. Acapulco was nestled behind them in the curve of the bay, its lights twinkling like a fairy town on display during the Christmas season. Dannee looked back, thinking how much the hotel reminded her of an Aztec temple, waiting for the human sacrifice. And the way she felt now, she was the sacrifice. She didn't look back again, but sat with hands clenched and eyes staring straight ahead.

Travis had knocked on her door at exactly eight o'clock. He had looked totally bored with the prospect of the party, and with her. He surveyed her impersonally, from the tie of her halter neckline to the tips of her sandaled feet, his eyes resting only for a second on her clenched hands, where the turquoise ring he had bought flashed with as much brightness as her eyes. Then he nodded his head as if he had been asked to pass judgment on her clothes. Silently, he had taken her arm and steered her toward the elevator. Dannee had thought of all kinds of comments, but all were put aside as she told herself that she could behave just as arrogantly as he could. Since then, silence had reigned.

"You won't succeed, you know."

Dannee lifted her chin. "Succeed at what?"

"You can't stay quiet much longer. Too many little speeches are rambling through your mind, dying to be expressed." He turned the wheel to follow another curve in the road. He was so assured, so in control!

"What makes you so sure of that, Mr. Cameron? No one gave you second sight, or the power to read minds," she ground out. "Just keep your suppositions to yourself and leave me to mine!" Her nerves were strung as tight as they would go. One more word and she was sure she would break into small pieces—or tears.

"I didn't think you could last long." Travis pressed his foot on the clutch and shifted to a lower gear, allowing the powerful car to coast down the steep grade.

Sudden rage spread through her, and without thinking, she raised her hand in an arc, but before she could slap him, Travis's hand was raised to ward her off.

"You little fool!" he grated as he braked, still gripping her wrist. The car stopped with a jerk at the foot of the hill and before she knew it, Dannee was wrapped in Travis's arms, held in a grip of steel as he forced her lips to his, devouring them. His mouth possessed hers, edging out all the fight, and leaving behind a feeling of lethargy. His other hand became lax, soothing her back before riding down to cup one perfect breast, teasing it to a blossoming fullness. She moaned, her arms wrapped around his waist, pulling him closer. She couldn't get enough. She wanted to feel him next to her, touching, teasing. There was no little voice telling her it was bad; it couldn't be, when it felt so right!

Travis reluctantly pulled away with a low groan. He deliberately sat her back in her seat. "You're the only woman I know who can make me so mad I lose control!"

"Is that what you were displaying? Your temper?"

He ran shaking hands through his dark hair, then straightened his tie as he watched a car bearing down on them through the rear-view mirror.

"I should have turned you over my knee." There was a grim twist to his lips as he surveyed her, once more drawn into his cool, cynical shell. "Freshen your lipstick, Dannee," he said, "and fix your hair. You look like you've been making love in the back seat of a car."

"Why you—" This time her hand connected with a crack, and she gasped as she realized what she had done. Her hand flew to her mouth, eyes wide as she watched his shocked expression turn to resignation.

"I—I'm sorry! But, you shouldn't have said that!" she stammered.

"You're right," he answered quietly. "It seems we can't do anything but shoot sparks off one another."

The car drove past them and honked its horn. Travis waved, then let the brake up and shifted into gear, following it.

Dannee glanced at him through her lashes. His profile was harsh, commanding, just as it had been when they first met. But was it? Somehow, he looked more saddened, more lonely than she had ever thought possible. She wanted so terribly to touch him, to wipe the frown from his brow, to watch his now stern mouth part in a smile.

Not another word was said as they continued up the small, winding road. They went another mile before Travis turned to the left and drove down someone's private driveway. By the time they reached the entrance of the large, sprawling home, Dannee had replaced her smeared lipstick and run a comb through her hair. They parked on the side, with the other cars, but before Dannee could reach for the door Travis stopped her.

"You can leave tomorrow, Dannee. Your pay will be waiting for you at the desk in the morning. I believe there's an eleven-thirty flight you can catch." His voice rang with finality.

Leave! Tomorrow! She sat, stunned, as she attempted to absorb the fact that Travis didn't even want her around for another day. She nodded her head automatically, afraid to try her tightened vocal cords. She had known her time with Travis was almost over, but somehow she still hadn't expected it to end. She didn't want to leave him! She wanted to stay, no matter what. She'd be his mistress, his plaything, whatever he wanted. She didn't care.

He came around the car and opened her door, helping her out. His touch was completely impersonal. He dropped his hand the minute she got her balance on the graveled driveway, and they turned, walking to the door of what looked like a large, one-story home. Dark, heavily carved double doors were framed by a rock alcove, and as Travis pushed the door open, ushering her in, the music blared out at them. He had been here before, if opening doors without knocking was any indication. Dannee's heart sank even further as she remembered who lived here. They stepped into the hall, which was actually a terrazzo-tiled balcony, overlooking an immense two-story den. Glass rose up from ground level to ceiling, giving the most beautiful view of Acapulco Bay at night that

Dannee had ever seen. The house had obviously been built into a hill, with only one story showing from the front.

It seemed that Teresa Martinez was not only beautiful, but obviously had the benefit of a rich father. Winding steps led down on both sides of the balcony to the floor below, where several couples gyrated to the recorded beat of a new rock group, while others stood in groups around the built-in bar and the first level patio.

The decor was contemporary, stark white and shades of iridescent blues with just a splash of bright orange here and there. The effect was stunning.

"Rather an eyeful," Travis commented, dryly.

Before Dannee could retort, she saw Teresa Martinez draw away from a group and walk toward the bottom of the stairs, awaiting their descent. Her sparkling black eyes were for Travis only, totally ignoring Dannee walking down the steps beside him.

"Travis! I was beginning to worry!" she cooed in a husky voice, her Latin accent added to her provocative glances. "Especially when you promised you wouldn't be late."

Dannee thought Teresa's silver lamé dress was too tight and much too obvious, but reflected that most men didn't seem to mind at all, especially Travis, if the devilish light in his eyes was anything to go by. Dannee had never been self-conscious about her figure before, but seeing the other woman in that dress made her realize just how nondescript she really was. They reached the bottom step and Travis immediately released Dannee's arm, leaving her holding the smooth, white wrought-iron banister. She couldn't hear Travis's comment, which made the lady chuckle, but Dannee just bet honey was dripping from his mouth as he took Teresa's arm and smiled down at her. Who would guess that a scant five minutes ago he had shattered Dannee's dreams into smithereens? Not that he knew—not that he would ever know.

Travis was a courteous date, however, considering the way he so obviously felt about her. He introduced Dannee to the men who had helped him put the grocery deal together, allowing her to put faces to the names she had been typing all week. But after handing her a large wineglass filled with a ruby-red, semi-sweet wine punch, he found her a comfortable seat on a cushion near the fireplace, then walked off with his hostess. Dannee had never felt more like a parked car in her life. Nothing else could have underlined the fact that he was through with her as much as his desertion at that moment.

She sat quietly, sipping her drink and pretending she was having the time of her life— all alone. She had a lifetime to cry, Dannee repeated to herself over and over, so why bother to start now?

"We men really can be nasty, can't we?" a deep, gravelly voice declared next to Dannee.

She looked up, startled. "I beg your pardon?"

The man nodded his head toward Travis and Teresa. "Your boyfriend. If I didn't know better, I'd say he was making a pass at Teresa."

Dannee followed his glance, only to see Travis take the dark beauty in his arms as a slow, dreamy love song began playing on the stereo. He was saying something to her and her head was tilted toward his, her lips puckered in a seductive pout. A shaft of pain flew through Dannee's heart. She looked back into the contents of her glass, not wanting to see them kiss. "He's not my boyfriend."

"Aren't you the one Travis kept here as his secretary?"

She shook her head, watching him warily now. Somehow, he looked vaguely familiar. "I'm the stand-in. His regular secretary's sick." Dannee stared at him a moment longer. "Do I know you?" she asked hesitantly.

He grinned, and with each shiny tooth, seemed more and more familiar to her.

Dannee gasped. "You're Noel Prescott!"

His grin widened, making his face seem younger and more boyish than his sixty-odd years. He had been *the* leading man in her mother's time and had, consequently, been the first leading man Dannee had ever wanted to see, too. His good looks and boyish charm had made him a hit with all generations. She remembered hearing about his stormy marriages to two sex goddesses before marrying a much younger actress in his later years. She hadn't heard anything about him since. Dannee didn't even think he had made any movies in the past four or five years.

Carefully, he lifted one pants leg so it would keep the crease, and placed his foot on the low fireplace, leaning his elbow to rest on his knee. "I didn't think someone as young as you are would recognize an old codger like me." His eyes twinkled merrily, unabashedly detailing her attributes, but she paid no attention.

"But of course I do! I remember my mother keeping up with your life, dragging me to films, reading everything that had your name in it," Dannee exclaimed.

"Ouch! I guess time passed faster than I realized," he groaned wryly. "I keep forgetting just how long it's been since I made my first picture." The smile disappeared momentarily, before he took a deep swig from his glass.

"I'm sorry, I didn't mean it to sound that way. Travis says I always say the first thing that pops into my head."

"And so you should. I knew someone like that once. It took me a long time to realize that what I called lack of tact was the only thing that kept my ego from getting too inflated. It was really just good old-fashioned plain talk. It makes a refreshing change from the movie industry, believe me!"

"Well, if it's any consolation, I saw *Autumn Love* three times, cried through each one and swore I'd never see another movie better than that one." Dannee smiled, dimpling.

"If it's any consolation to you, young lady, I saw it twice as many times and thought it was my best effort, too. Of course, the actress I worked with, Andrea Newcomb, wasn't any slouch, either."

"Whatever happened to her?"

His face projected a sadness that squeezed Dannee's heart. "She died last year."

Of course! That was the young starlet he had married and disappeared into the sunset with! "She was very beautiful, just the way a leading lady should be," Dannee said, softly. "She didn't look like she'd spill drinks in your lap, or step on your foot," she added wistfully, trying hard to ignore the couple swirling around the dance floor.

Travis and Teresa made a beautiful twosome, Dannee observed sadly. Both were dark with beautifully tanned skin, and Teresa was tiny enough to make Travis seem even stronger and larger, if that was possible.

Confusion was stamped all over the actor's face, but only for a moment, as he followed the path of Dannee's eyes. "I see." He cleared his throat, then removed his foot from the hearth and seated himself on the cushion next to Dannee. "So that's how it is with you?"

Dannee nodded her head, trying not to let the tears fall down her cheeks. What was the matter with her anyway? She had never behaved so stupidly in her life! And to top it off, here she was, telling a world famous actor her problems! At least, she thought, if I'm foolish enough to be miserable, I pick good company while I'm at it!

She gave Noel Prescott a watery smile, not quite looking into his eyes. She couldn't stand to see pity, especially for herself.

"Well, cheer up, my girl. It hasn't been that long ago that I don't remember what it's like myself. Love can be pretty terrible sometimes, but at least it beats not feeling anything at all. Besides, I've found from experience that the pain may not go away, but at least it dulls."

"Thanks." She sipped her drink once more.

The music stopped and Travis and Teresa parted, laughing at some private joke as they walked off the floor—toward Dannee.

"Do you dance?" Dannee asked hurriedly, glancing up at the actor as if he had just spouted the most profound words of wisdom.

He was taken aback for just a moment, before smiling an answer. "Of course I do! And I love dancing with beautiful women. Would you do me the honor?"

He stood, holding out his hand. She placed her hand in his and they walked to the middle of the floor, completely ignoring the couple standing nearby, waiting to be acknowledged.

While they danced, Noel told anecdotes about everyone he knew in the movie industry. People whose names Dannee had heard and revered all her life were mentioned, and the stories made them seem human as only an insider's tales could. Before she knew it, the song was coming to a close, but they continued to stand on the dance floor as Noel finished his story.

"And then he put his hand on his hip and his nose in the air and said 'My dear Claudia, if wishes were horses, then I'd ride to the East!'"

They both laughed with the ease of two old friends enjoying each other's company. It seemed strange to Dannee that someone she had imagined as being so suave, so continental, could also be so warm and human.

"I believe it's my dance." Travis stood next to Dannee, his face stern.

"To this music?" Dannee exclaimed as a loud, disco tune blared through the wall speakers.

She glanced around, watching a few of the others walking onto the floor; then her eye moved toward the turntable—and Teresa. The other woman's hands were coming off the dials as she turned and surveyed the threesome still standing on what had been designated the dance floor. If looks could kill . . . , thought Dannee. "Thank you, I think I'll pass," she retorted stiffly.

Travis turned and walked away without another word.

Dannee followed Noel off the floor. They resumed their seats on the fireplace while Noel continued to regale her with talk of the movie industry. He was obviously trying hard to keep her mind off Travis and the fact that he had disappeared with Teresa twenty minutes ago.

Finally, he pushed a bowl of peanuts under her nose while he spoke. "I had a wife," he said, suddenly serious, "either number one or number two. And every time we had an argument, she headed for the refrigerator. Then she'd return shaking celery, or carrots, or scallions under my nose, while she continued with her side of the debate."

Dannee gave a shaky smile. "Is that why you divorced her?"

"No. I divorced her because she couldn't manage the food budget on the amount of money I gave her," Noel quipped, but he had lost her attention again, for Travis had returned and was standing at the bar.

Teresa isn't with him, but she can't be far away, Dannee thought.

Travis turned slowly, a drink in his hand as his eyes surveyed the room without interest.

Dannee grabbed for the bowl of peanuts. "They look good. I think I'll—oops!"

As her hands touched the rim of the bowl, it overturned, spilling the contents into Noel Prescott's lap. Salt and peanut skins clung to his slacks as peanuts rolled down his tailored pant legs onto the floor.

"I'm so sorry!" Dannee exclaimed, tears once more welling up. "I don't know what the problem is, but I don't think I'd better return to Acapulco. It must be something in the water!" She mumbled the last as she reached down, trying to catch the rolling nuts before someone stepped on them.

She was on her hands and knees, scooping them into a small pile, when she noticed dark brown Italian leather shoes standing in front of her, and her heart began double-thumping on cue.

Slowly, her eyes followed the crease of his pants and by the time she reached Travis's face she was as angry as he was. How dare he judge her! She hadn't wanted to come to this stupid party in the first place!

"Would you mind moving?" she asked caustically. "You're making a bigger mess by crushing them!"

"Get up!" His face was rigid, teeth clenched, and she did the only thing she could do under the circumstances. She stood up.

"Excuse us," Travis muttered to Noel over his shoulder.

Then he grabbed Dannee's arm, almost jerking her off her feet as he pulled her after him toward the patio doors at the end of the room.

Dannee shot a pleading glance toward Noel Prescott, but he just sat there by the fireplace, beaming like a happy buddha. Men! Were they all anger and imbecilic smiles?

Travis jerked her arm again, ignoring the surprised stares of the guests closest to the door. He propelled her onto the patio, then down the winding steps to the level below.

Tropical plants surrounded a kidney-shaped

pool which looked more like a movie setting than something real. He led her to a low rock wall where an alcove was formed by more tropical greenery. He stopped, jerked her arm again, neatly maneuvering her into his arms.

"You certainly know your way around, caveman!" Dannee exploded, her arms on his shoulders as she tried to keep her balance. "And what will your hostess think of you dragging me out here to view the stars?"

"Forget Teresa! I have! You're a witch, do you know that? How one small woman can make me so angry, I'll never understand!" he growled, his hands tightening around her hips to bring her closer to the muscled length of him.

"I resent that! I've tried to stay out of your way all evening so you could have a clear field in which to pursue your *señorita,* and I am *not* small! She is!"

"Shut up!" His lips came down hard, parting and exploring the moist sweetness of her mouth with an urgency that was overpowering. Almost immediately, his anger dissolved, turning punishment into warm, wonderful torture.

He held her so tight that Dannee could hardly breathe, pressing her to him as if he wanted her to dissolve against him. She gave up trying to fight. She wanted his kisses, his touch, as much as he seemed to want her, at least for this moment. Her hands wandered down his shoulders to his chest, unbuttoning his shirt so she could slip her hands over his taut skin. He groaned, and she delighted in the pleasure she aroused.

"How do you do it?" he asked hoarsely. "How do you keep me wanting you so much I ache at night and can't think of anything else all day but holding you like this, making love to you under a golden moon."

"Then, you'd better take me," she laughed, breathless, hardly aware of what she was saying.

"What did you say?" Travis held her away without letting her go, searching her face in the moonlight for a confirmation of what he had just heard.

Suddenly, Dannee wanted to retreat, she was too vulnerable, too exposed.

Travis's hands left her waist as he buttoned his shirt.

Dannee turned, facing the pool rather than face Travis. They stood on a stone balcony that looked like it was the middle tier of three balconies connected by steep, rock steps. This level held the kidney-shaped pool with a gaily striped bathhouse of canvas, and a rock barbecue pit. All the levels overlooked Acapulco Bay, but Dannee wasn't interested in the scenery, only in the man who was now standing with one foot on the low wall as he bent against the wind and lit a cigarette. She could see his harsh features by flamelight, then there was nothing but the glow of the tip of his cigarette.

"Excuse me," she mumbled and turned

sharply toward the steps. She could get a cab to come fetch her, or perhaps catch a ride with one of the other guests. If necessary, she could walk, but she had to get away!

"Where do you think you're going?" Travis's hand snaked out, holding her where she stood.

"Isn't that just like a man!" She choked on her laugh. "Offer him what he says he wants and he decides he doesn't want it anymore—until it's taken away!" She twisted her hand, but Travis wouldn't let her go. "Well, it's my option, so if you don't mind, I think I'll take it and leave."

"The only place you're going is with me!" he declared, ominously.

Now it was her turn to be stunned. "What?"

"Perhaps I'll be able to get some work done if I have you with me all the time. At least then I won't have to worry about you spilling things on other men!"

"I didn't spill on purpose!" she exclaimed. "But I looked up and saw you staring at me and I had to do something! When I reached for the nuts, I wasn't really seeing them. I only saw that look on your face! So, you see," Dannee accused, irrationally, "it was all your fault!"

Travis grinned and his white teeth gleamed against his dark, tanned skin. "That's a relief. I thought I'd been replaced in your affections by that aging Romeo."

He arced his cigarette over the low wall as he turned to face her. His hand left her wrist to rest on her slight shoulders, one hand caressing the nape of her neck, sending tingling messages through the rest of her body.

"Please," she begged, "let me go! I'll get a ride back to the hotel and be out of your life tomorrow."

His hands tightened. "You'll never be out of my life. We're getting married as soon as possible. Tonight, if I can arrange it!" he stated imperiously.

Confusion reigned in Dannee's mind. "You want to marry me because I embarrass you by spilling things?"

"I want to marry you. Period."

"Do I have anything to say in the matter?"

"No."

She hesitated. With the wonderful and exciting message that he wanted her, perhaps even loved her as she loved him, came the reminder of Miranda, sitting on the edge of the bed and speaking of her wedding.

"Miranda is marrying the man she should have married a year ago," Travis said, reading her mind. "He's a good friend of mine, by the way. They were engaged, then Tony was wounded in Viet Nam. He came back blind and didn't want to hold Miranda to her promise to marry him. And she was too timid to push for what she really wanted—him!

"Two weeks ago, she saw him again and realized just how much she loved him. When she was ill, she had a lot of time to think, and decided to tell him what she had known all along, that she loved him, no matter what. She called him then, and when Tony realized she really did love him, he asked Miranda to marry him right away. She'd been carrying his ring with her all this time, and she was only too happy to put it back on."

"But why didn't you tell me?"

"Because it was Miranda's private life. I was going to tell you as soon as she made up her mind, but I didn't know myself until I walked into her room and found you rolling curses off your tongue—and I was the recipient."

"You could have explained."

"I started to, but my pride stood in the way. I asked you to take our relationship on faith, but you chose not to."

"Then—you two aren't engaged, and she isn't in love with you?" Dannee murmured wonderingly. Who could help being in love with Travis?

"If she is, she never said a word about it to me."

Travis folded Dannee in his arms, gently holding her as if she were fragile porcelain. "And it wouldn't matter anyway. Because I'm in love with *you*, and I'm not letting you go—ever! So you might as well resign yourself. All the others will have to find someone else. I've known from the first that you were mine, but I had to give you time to realize it, too. Teresa was just a way of speeding up your decision. So are you mine, Dannee?"

"I'm yours . . . always," Dannee dreamily confirmed.

"You're my dream, Dannee. I've wandered

for years, trying to find someone like you. And now that I have you, you'll never get away! I won't let you!" He kissed her again.

"And if I ever catch you dumping anything on any other man, I'll beat you within an inch of your life. Do you understand me, Dannee?" His voice held only mock anger and his eyes held the promise of all the years to come.

"If you ever again have an overwhelming urge to spill, I'll be right next to you. It will be me, and no one else, who receives your 'favors.' Understand?"

"Yes, sir." she answered subserviently, the merriment in her eyes belying the tone of her voice.

"You witch . . ." he growled, and his lips found hers with unspoken, bright promises of tomorrow—promises as bright as the Acapulco sunsets. . . .

IT'S YOUR OWN SPECIAL TIME

Contemporary romances for today's women.

Each month, six very special love stories will be yours

from SILHOUETTE.

Look for them wherever books are sold

or order now from the coupon below.

$1.50 each

Silhouette Romance

___#55 WINTER'S HEART Ladame

___#56 RISING STAR Trent

___#57 TO TRUST TOMORROW John

___#58 LONG WINTER'S NIGHT Stanford

___#59 KISSED BY MOONLIGHT Vernon

___#60 GREEN PARADISE Hill

___#61 WHISPER MY NAME Michaels

___#62 STAND-IN BRIDE Halston

___#63 SNOWFLAKES IN THE SUN Brent

___#64 SHADOW OF APOLLO Hampson

___#65 A TOUCH OF MAGIC Hunter

___#66 PROMISES FROM THE PAST Vitek

___#67 ISLAND CONQUEST Hastings

___#68 THE MARRIAGE BARGAIN Scott

___#69 WEST OF THE MOON St. George

___#70 MADE FOR EACH OTHER Afton Bonds

___#71 A SECOND CHANCE ON LOVE Ripy

___#72 ANGRY LOVER Beckman

___#73 WREN OF PARADISE Browning

___#74 WINTER DREAMS Trent

___#75 DIVIDE THE WIND Carroll

___#76 BURNING MEMORIES Hardy

___#77 SECRET MARRIAGE Cork

___#78 DOUBLE OR NOTHING Oliver

___#79 TO START AGAIN Helldorson

___#80 WONDER AND WILD DESIRE Stephens

___#81 IRISH THOROUGHBRED Roberts

___#82 THE HOSTAGE BRIDE Dailey

___#83 LOVE LEGACY Halston

___#84 VEIL OF GOLD Vitek

___#85 OUTBACK SUMMER John

___#86 THE MOTH AND THE FLAME Adams

___#87 BEYOND TOMORROW Michaels

___#88 AND THEN CAME DAWN Stanford

___#89 A PASSIONATE BUSINESS James

___#90 WILD LADY Major

___#91 WRITTEN IN THE STARS Hunter

___#92 DESERT DEVIL McKay

___#93 EAST OF TODAY Browning

___#94 ENCHANTMENT Hampson

___#95 FOURTEEN KARAT BEAUTY Wisdom

___#96 LOVE'S TREACHEROUS JOURNEY Beckman

___#97 WANDERER'S DREAM Clay

___#98 MIDNIGHT WINE St. George

___#99 TO HAVE, TO HOLD Camp

SILHOUETTE BOOKS, Department SB/1
1230 Avenue of the Americas
New York, NY 10020

Please send me the books I have checked above. I am enclosing
$_____ (please add 50¢ to cover postage and handling. NYS and
NYC residents please add appropriate sales tax). Send check or
money order—no cash or C.O.D.'s please. Allow six weeks for delivery.

NAME_____

ADDRESS_____

CITY_____STATE/ZIP_____

Silhouette *Romance*

15-Day Free Trial Offer
6 Silhouette Romances

6 Silhouette Romances, free for 15 days! We'll send you 6 new Silhouette Romances to keep for 15 days, absolutely free! If you decide not to keep them, send them back to us. You pay nothing.

Free Home Delivery. But if you enjoy them as much as we think you will, keep them by paying us the retail price of just $1.50 each. We'll pay all shipping and handling charges. You'll then automatically become a member of the Silhouette Book Club, and will receive 6 more new Silhouette Romances every month and a bill for $9.00. That's the same price you'd pay in the store, but you get the convenience of home delivery.

Read every book we publish. The Silhouette Book Club is the way to make sure you'll be able to receive every new romance we publish.

READERS' COMMENTS ON SILHOUETTE ROMANCES:

"Your books are written with so much feeling and quality that they make you feel as if you are part of the story."

—D.C.*, Piedmont, SC

"I'm very particular about the types of romances I read; yours more than fill my thirst for reading."

—C.D., Oxford, MI

"I hope Silhouette novels stay around for many years to come. . . . Keep up the good work."

—P.C., Frederick, MD

"What a relief to be able to escape in a well-written romantic story."

—E.N.. Santa Maria, CA

"Silhouette Romances . . . Fantastic!"

—M.D., Bell, CA

"I'm pleased to be adding your books to my collection—my library is growing in size every day."

—B.L., La Crescenta, CA

* Names available on request.